♠♥ 不朽奇幻童話經典 ♠♥

愛麗絲鏡中奇遇

Through the Looking-Glass

中英雙語版

路易斯·凱洛——著
約翰·田尼爾——繪
廖綉玉————譯

晨星出版

愛藏本088

愛麗絲鏡中奇遇【中英雙語版】
Through the Looking-Glass

作　　者｜路易斯·凱洛（Lewis Carroll）
繪　　者｜約翰·田尼爾（John Tenniel）
譯　　者｜廖綉玉

責任編輯｜林儀涵
封面設計｜黃裴文
美術編輯｜黃寶慧

創 辦 人｜陳銘民
發 行 所｜晨星出版有限公司
　　　　　台中市407工業區30路1號
　　　　　TEL：04-23595820　FAX：04-23550581
　　　　　E-mail: service@morningstar.com.tw
　　　　　http://www.morningstar.com.tw
　　　　　行政院新聞局局版台業字第2500號
法律顧問｜陳思成律師
郵政劃撥｜22326758（晨星出版有限公司）
服務專線｜04-23595819#230

印　　刷｜承毅印刷股份有限公司

出版日期｜2016年04月30日1刷
定　　價｜新台幣250元
ISBN 978-986-443-115-1
Printed in Taiwan
All Right Reserved
版權所有·翻印必究
如有缺頁或破損，請寄回更換

國家圖書館出版品預行編目資料

愛麗絲鏡中奇遇 / 路易斯·凱洛（Lewis Carroll）著；廖綉玉譯
臺中市：晨星，2016.04
愛藏本；88
譯自：Through the Looking-Glass
ISBN 978-986-443-115-1（平裝）
CIP 873.59　105001899

愛麗絲鏡中奇遇・目錄

THROUGH THE LOOKING-GLASS

第一章　鏡中屋　006

第二章　活花的花園　028

第三章　鏡中昆蟲　046

第四章　崔德頓和崔德迪　062

第五章　羊毛與水　087

第六章　蛋頭先生　107

第七章　獅子與獨角獸　130

第八章　「這是我的發明」

第九章　愛麗絲王后

第十章　搖晃

第十一章　醒來

第十二章　誰做的夢？

203　　202　　201　　174　　148

第一章　鏡中屋

有一點可以確定：這件事跟小白貓毫無關聯，完全是小黑貓的錯，因為從十五分鐘前到現在，貓媽媽一直在幫小白貓洗臉（說真的，小白貓算是很乖了），所以小白貓根本不可能插手搗蛋。

貓媽媽黛娜是這樣幫孩子洗臉的：牠先用一隻爪子按住小傢伙的耳朵往下壓，再用另一隻爪子從鼻子開始逆毛幫牠擦整張臉。現在呢，就像我說的，黛娜正忙著幫小白貓擦臉，小白貓乖乖躺著不動，偶爾發出呼嚕聲，顯然知道這都是為了牠好。

但是小黑貓這天下午稍早就洗過臉了，所以當愛麗絲蜷在大扶手椅的一角，喃喃自語又半睡半醒時，小黑貓就趁機把愛麗絲努力捲到一半的毛線球當成玩

具，玩得不亦樂乎，牠把毛線球滾來滾去，最後毛線球整個散開了，毛線在壁爐前的地毯上亂成一團，小黑貓就在毛線堆裡追著自己的尾巴轉圈。

愛麗絲大喊：「喔，你這個小壞蛋！」她抓起小黑貓，輕輕吻了一下，「說真的，黛娜應該多教你一點規矩的！」愛麗絲用責備的眼神看著貓媽媽，裝出惱怒的聲音說：「黛娜，你真的應該多教牠一點規矩，你知道你該教牠的！」接著愛麗絲抱著小黑貓，撿起毛線，爬回扶手椅，重新開始捲毛線球，但捲得不快，因為

她講個不停，有時對小黑貓講，有時對自己講。小黑貓凱蒂故作正經地坐在愛麗絲的膝上，假裝認真看她捲毛線球，不時伸出爪子輕輕碰一碰毛線球，彷彿愛麗絲允許的話，牠很樂意幫忙。

愛麗絲開始說：「凱蒂，你知道明天是什麼日子嗎？如果你剛剛跟我一起待在窗邊，就猜得到了，只是那時候黛娜正在幫你洗臉，所以你猜不到。我看到那些男孩在撿樹枝，準備生營火。凱蒂，那需要很多樹枝呢！只是天氣變得好冷，雪又那麼大，所以他們不得不停下來。沒關係，凱蒂，我們明天再去看營火。」說到這裡，愛麗絲拿起毛線在小黑貓的脖子上繞了兩三圈，看好不好看，結果搞得一團亂，毛線球滾到地板上，長長的毛線再度散開了。

愛麗絲與小黑貓再度舒舒服服坐回扶手椅，愛麗絲繼續說：「凱蒂，你知道嗎？我真的很生氣！當我看到你做的這些惡作劇時，差點就要打開窗戶把你扔到外面的雪地裡！你活該受罰，你這個調皮的小可愛！還有什麼話好說？現在別插嘴！」愛麗絲豎起一根手指頭接著說：「我要把你做錯的事一一告訴

你，第一件：今天早上黛娜幫你洗臉的時候，你尖叫了兩次，凱蒂，你抵賴不了，我都聽到了！你說什麼？（她假裝小黑貓在說話。）她的爪子戳到你的眼睛？嗯，那是你的錯，你不該睜開眼睛，如果你把眼睛閉起來，就不會發生這種事了。好了，別再找藉口，聽我說！第二件：我把一碟牛奶放在雪兒面前的時候，你硬拉牠的尾巴把牠拉走了！什麼？你口渴？那你又怎麼知道她不渴呢？現在說第三件：你趁我不注意的時候，把毛線球全部弄散了！」

「凱蒂，這就是你做錯的三件事，我都還沒懲罰你呢，我要把你該受的處罰全部都累積起來，下星期三再一起算帳。如果他們也把我的處罰累積起來算總帳，那該怎麼辦？」與其說愛麗絲是在對小貓說話，不如說是自言自語，「到了年底，他們會怎麼做呢？我猜我應該會被送進監獄吧，讓我想一想，或許每次的處罰都是不准吃晚餐，那麼等到悲慘的年底，我就得連續餓五十頓了！哼，我才沒那麼在意！我寧可少吃五十頓晚餐，也不要一口氣吃進五十頓晚餐！」

「凱蒂，你有沒有聽見雪花落在玻璃窗上的聲音？多麼美妙輕柔的聲音啊！好像有人在外頭親吻整片窗子。我想知道雪花是不是很愛那些樹木與田野，所以才會這麼溫柔地親吻它們？接著再幫它們舒舒服服蓋上一條白色被子，也許還會說：『親愛的，睡吧，睡到夏天來臨吧！』凱蒂呀，等到它們在夏天甦醒，就會穿上一身綠，風兒一吹就隨風起舞。喔，那多美呀！」愛麗絲拍手大聲讚嘆，毛線球又掉了，「我真希望這一切都是真的！我很確定秋天時樹葉都變起來昏昏欲睡。」

「凱蒂，你會下棋嗎？喔，親愛的，別笑了，我是認真問的，因為剛才我們下棋時，你好像看得懂，我喊『將軍！』時，你還呼嚕了一聲！嗯，凱蒂，我那一步走得真棒，要不是那個討厭的騎士半途衝向我的棋子，我可能真的就贏了。凱蒂，親愛的，我們來假裝……」愛麗絲常常掛在嘴邊的話很多，我連一半都講不完，她最愛的口頭禪就是「我們來假裝」。昨天愛麗絲與姐姐爭論很久，因為她說：「我們來假裝是國王們與王后們。」她姐姐是個很嚴謹的

人，說她們無法同時假裝成那麼多人，因為她們只有兩個人。愛麗絲最好只好說：「好吧，那你假裝成其中一個，其他的都由我來假裝。」還有一次愛麗絲突然在老奶媽耳邊大喊：「奶媽！我們來假裝我是飢餓的土狼，你是骨頭！」這讓奶媽嚇了一大跳。

不過這扯遠了，還是回到愛麗絲對小貓咪說的話吧。

「凱蒂，我們來假裝你是紅棋王后！我覺得你要是坐起來，兩隻手臂交叉，看起來就跟她一模一樣。來，試試吧，乖！」愛麗絲拿起桌上的紅棋王后，把它豎在凱蒂面前讓牠模仿，但沒成功，愛麗絲說主要是因為凱蒂不肯交叉抱著兩隻手臂。所以，愛麗絲為了處罰凱蒂，就把牠抱起來照鏡子，讓牠看看牠繃著臉的模樣，愛麗絲補了一句：「如果你不乖乖聽話，我就把你丟到鏡中屋裡，你覺得怎麼樣？」

「好了，凱蒂，如果你專心聽，別那麼多話，我就把我知道的鏡中屋告訴你。首先，透過鏡子你會看見一個房間，那就跟我們的客廳一模一樣，只是所

愛麗絲鏡中奇遇　012

有東西都跟我們的左右相反。如果我站在椅子上，就能看到那個房間全部的模樣，只有壁爐後面的地方看不到。喔，我真希望能看到那邊！我真想知道他們冬天的時候是不是生火來取暖，不過這根本就無法分辨，除非我們的壁爐生火冒煙，那個房間的壁爐裡也才會跟著冒煙，但或許那是假的，只是為了讓那個壁爐看起來有火而已。那個房間裡的書跟我們的書很像，只是字都反了，我很清楚這件事，因為我曾經把一本書拿到鏡子前面，那個房間裡的他們也拿起一本書。」

「凱蒂，你想不想住在鏡中屋啊？不知道他們會不會給你牛奶喝？搞不好鏡中屋的牛奶不好喝。喔，凱蒂！我們看到鏡中屋的走廊了，如果把我們客廳的門敞開，就能稍微瞥到鏡中屋的走廊，你看到的走廊就跟我們的走廊很像，但說不定再過去就完全不一樣。喔，凱蒂！如果我們可以穿過鏡子，走入鏡中屋，那一定很棒！我敢說那邊一定有很多漂亮東西！凱蒂，我們來假裝有條路可以通到鏡中屋，我們來假裝鏡子變得像薄紗一樣軟，這樣我們就能穿過去

了。哎呀，它真的變成
薄霧了，天啊！我們很
容易就能穿過去⋯⋯」

愛麗絲說話時，已經爬
上壁爐臺了，儘管她不
知道自己是怎麼爬上去
的。鏡子真的開始融化
了，就像一層亮銀色的
薄霧。

　　愛麗絲一下子就鑽
過去了，接著她輕輕跳
下壁爐臺，來到鏡中的
房間。

她做的第一件事就
是看看壁爐裡有沒有
火，她很高興地發現裡
面真的有火，爐火熊熊
燃燒，就跟原來客廳的
爐火燒得一樣旺。

愛麗絲心想：「這
樣一來的話，我就像在
原來的客廳裡一樣暖
和，其實更暖和，因為
這邊沒有人會罵我，叫
我不要太靠近火。喔，
如果他們透過鏡子看到

我在這邊，又抓不到我，那真是太好玩了！」

愛麗絲開始東張西望，她注意到一件事：她在原來客廳看得到的鏡中屋部分都很普通無趣，但看不到的地方就非常不同。

例如壁爐旁邊牆上掛的畫看起來都是活的，壁爐臺上的那座時鐘正面是小老頭的臉（你從鏡子裡只能看到時鐘的背面），朝她咧嘴笑。

愛麗絲注意到壁爐灰燼裡有幾個棋子，她心想：「他們沒把這邊的客廳打掃得像我們那邊一樣乾淨。」但

片刻後，她發出「喔」的驚叫聲，趴跪在地上看著這些棋子，這些棋子正兩個兩個一對，四處散步呢！

愛麗絲說（輕聲細語，怕嚇到它們）：「這是紅棋國王與紅棋王后，坐在鏟子邊緣上的是白棋國王與白棋王后，兩個城堡棋牽手散步。我覺得它們聽不到我說話，」她低下頭，越來越靠近棋子，繼續說：「我幾乎可以確定它們看不見我。我好像變成隱形人……」

這時，愛麗絲背後的桌上有東西開始驚聲尖叫，她轉頭正好看見一個白棋士兵滾倒了，雙腳開始亂踢。愛麗絲非常好奇地盯著它，看看接下來會發生什麼事情。

白棋王后大喊：「那是我孩子的聲音！」白棋王后從白棋國王身邊衝過去，衝勁很猛，白棋國王被撞倒在煤灰裡。「我的寶貝莉莉！我的小公主！」

她開始攀著壁爐柵欄瘋狂往上爬。

白棋國王揉揉摔痛的鼻子說：「見鬼的小公主！」他有權對王后生一點

氣，因為他從頭到腳都沾上灰燼。

愛麗絲急著想幫忙，可憐的小莉莉尖叫到快昏倒了，愛麗絲連忙拿起白棋王后放到桌上，放在她吵鬧不休的小女兒旁邊。

白棋王后喘著氣，坐了下來，這趟飛速的空中之旅嚇得她喘不過氣。有一兩分鐘之久她只是靜靜抱著她的小莉莉，什麼也做不了，等她稍微喘過氣來，就朝著坐在灰燼裡生氣的白棋國王大喊：「小心火山！」

白棋國王說：「什麼火山？」他憂慮地望著爐火，彷彿認為那是最有可能找到火山的地方。

白棋王后喘著氣說：「它……把……我……噴……上……來。」她還是有點喘不過氣，「上來的時候要留心，照正常的方式，別被噴上來了！」

愛麗絲看著白棋國王辛苦地攀著柵欄往上爬，最後她說：「哎呀，照這樣的速度，你要爬好幾個小時才能爬上桌子。我最好還是幫幫你，對吧？」但白棋國王根本沒注意到她問的問題，顯然聽不到她說話，也看不見她。

愛麗絲輕輕拿起白棋國王，慢慢地移動，速度比剛才拿起白棋王后時來得慢，免得把他嚇得喘不過氣。但就在愛麗絲準備把白棋國王放到桌上之前，她覺得應該幫他撣一撣，因為他全身是灰。

後來愛麗絲說，她一輩子從沒見過白棋國王當時那種表情。他發現自己被隱形的手抓到空中，全身的灰還被撣掉，他嚇得叫都叫不出來，但眼睛與嘴巴越張越大，越來越圓。愛麗絲大笑，手一抖，差點害他掉到地上。

愛麗絲大聲說：「喔！親愛的，拜託別做出這種表情！」她忘了白棋國王根本聽不到她說話，「你讓我笑得差點拿不住你了！嘴巴別張得那麼大！灰燼會跑進去的。好了，我想你現在夠乾淨了！」她順一順白棋國王的頭髮，接著

把他放在桌上的白棋王后旁邊。

白棋國王立刻仰天躺下，一動也不動。愛麗絲看見自己幹的好事，有點嚇到了，她在客廳裡四處尋找，看看能不能找點水潑醒他。但她找不到水，只找到一瓶墨水。

她帶著墨水回來時，發現白棋國王已經醒了，他與白棋王后驚慌地竊竊私語，聲音壓得很低，愛麗絲幾乎聽不到他們說的話。

白棋國王說：「親愛的，相信我，我嚇得全身發冷，就連鬍子的尾端都變冷了！」

白棋王后回答：「你根本沒有鬍子。」

白棋國王繼續說：「那恐怖的時刻，我永遠、永遠都不會忘記！」

白棋王后說：「可是如果你不把這件事寫下來的話，你一定會忘記的。」

白棋國王從口袋裡拿出一本巨大的筆記本，開始寫了起來，愛麗絲興致勃勃地在一旁觀看。

她忽然冒出一個念頭，接著抓住鉛筆末端（鉛筆高過白棋國王的肩膀），開始幫他寫字。

可憐的白棋國王一臉困惑，看起來很不高興。他默默跟鉛筆搏鬥片刻，但愛麗絲的力氣比他大得多，最後他氣喘吁吁地說：「我的天啊！我真的必須找一支細一點的鉛筆來寫，我根本就沒辦法控制這枝筆，它寫的東西都不是我想寫的……」

白棋王后說：「它寫了什麼東西？」她瀏覽筆記本（愛麗絲寫的是：「白棋騎士從火鉗滑下來，無法保持平衡。」），然後接著說：「這根本就不是你的感想。」

愛麗絲身旁的桌子上擺了一本書，她盯著白棋國王的時候（因為她仍然有點擔心他，手裡拿著那瓶墨水，要是他又昏倒就能潑醒他），順手翻了幾頁，想找讀得懂的，她自言自語：「因為書上都是我看不懂的文字。」

書上的字就像這樣：

炳家罟不凿魯。

黽悲的在玺卓。

在圍苾劂轉镲镲：

炙窖之瓰。氙晶斁斁。

查對蕪基龘

她苦思片刻，但最後靈機一動，「哎呀，當然啦，這是鏡子裡的書啊！如果我把它拿到鏡子前面，顛倒的字就會變正了。」以下是愛麗絲讀到的詩⋯

查博蕪基龍

炙餐之刻，活滑類獾，

在圍緣螺轉錐鑽：

虛悲的布洛鳥，

迷家碧豕哨吼。

我兒啊，小心查博蕪基龍！

牠有啃咬的利齒，牠有抓攫的利爪！

還要小心啾布啾布鳥，

避開噴怒的邦德斯納獸！

他手持沃波寶劍：

尋找蠻森族的仇敵，

久了就在騰騰樹下歇息，

佇立思索片刻。

他思緒翻騰之時，

雙眼噴火的查博蕪基龍

間歇噴火，穿越吐爾基森林而來，

發出咩咩喃鳴聲。

得意洋洋把家還。

他提著龍首，拋下屍首，

沃波寶劍刺死巨龍！

一、二！一、二！刺了又刺，

你殺了查博蕪基龍？

我笑容滿面的兒子，到我懷裡來！

噢，多妙樂的日子！喀囉！喀勒！

他樂得咯咯笑。

炙餐之刻，活滑類獲，
在圍緣螺轉錐鑽⋯⋯
虛悲的布洛鳥，
迷家碧豕哨咆。

愛麗絲讀完後說：「這首詩好像很美，但非常難懂！（你看，她不想承認自己根本讀不懂，甚至不願對自己承認這一點。）讀完以後，我的腦袋似乎塞滿各種想法，只是我不知道究竟是什麼想法！反正是某人殺了某個東西，無論如何，這一點非常清楚⋯⋯」

愛麗絲忽然跳起來，她心想：「喔！我不快一點的話，還來不及看完這間鏡中屋的其他地方，就得穿過鏡子回去了！我先去看看花園吧！」她立刻衝出

客廳，沿著樓梯往下跑，或者其實不能說是奔跑，而是像愛麗絲對自己說的，那是她新發明的方法，下樓迅速又輕鬆，指尖沿著樓梯扶手，整個人輕輕飄下樓，雙腳甚至沒碰到樓梯。接著，她繼續飄過走廊，如果她沒及時抓住門柱，大概會直接飄出大門。她飄了一陣子，頭有點暈，等到她發現自己再度能用雙腳正常走路，相當開心。

想一想

你曾觀察過鏡子裡面的世界嗎？你看到的那個世界長什麼樣子？

第二章 活花的花園

愛麗絲自言自語：「如果我能走上那座小山的山頂，就能把這個花園看得更清楚，這裡有條小路可以直接到山頂……至少可以到……不，不行……」（她沿著那條小路走了好幾公尺，拐過幾個急轉彎）「但我想它最後還是通往山頂吧，可是這條小路彎得好

奇怪！它不像條路，反而像螺絲錐！嗯，我想轉過這個彎就會通往山上吧……

不，不對！這樣會直接回到房子前面了！好吧，我試試另一個方向。」

愛麗絲就這樣會走上走下，拐過一個又一個彎，但不管怎麼走，最後她總是回到房子前面。

事實上，有一次她比平常更快地轉過一個彎，結果來不及停步，直接撞上了房子。

愛麗絲說：「你講什麼都沒用！」她抬頭看著房子，假裝房子正與她爭辯，「現在我還不打算再進去，我知道我早晚得再度穿過鏡子，回到原來的客廳，然後這場冒險就結束了！」

所以她堅決地轉身背對房子，沿著小路再度出發，下定決心要直接走到山頂。有那麼幾分鐘，一切都很順利，愛麗絲說：「我這次真的會成功……」這時，小路忽然轉了個彎，（照愛麗絲後來的描述）還搖晃起來，緊接著她發現自己竟然走進了房子的大門。

愛麗絲大喊：「喔，真的太壞了！我從來沒看過這麼會擋路的房子！從來沒見過！」

然而，小山就在眼前，所以她也沒別的辦法，只好再次出發。這次她偶然發現一大片花圃，邊緣種了一圈雛菊，中間是一棵柳樹。

愛麗絲對著一朵優雅迎風搖曳的花兒說：「喔，虎皮百合！我真希望你會說話。」

虎皮百合說：「我們會說話啊，如果有人值得我們開口的話。」

愛麗絲嚇得一時說不出話來，似乎喘不過氣。最後，當虎皮百合又開始隨風搖曳，愛麗絲才以近乎耳語的音量，怯生生再度開口：「所有的花兒都會說話嗎？」

虎皮百合說：「說得就跟你一樣好，而且比你大聲多了。」

玫瑰說：「你知道的，我們先開口不禮貌，我剛剛才很好奇你何時才要開口呢！我對自己說：『她的臉看起來懂點道理，只是不太聰明而已！』不過你

的顏色不錯，那會很有用。」

虎皮百合評論說：「我才不在乎顏色呢，如果她的花瓣再捲一點，就會更好看。」

愛麗絲不喜歡被品頭論足，所以開始發問：「你們被種在這裡，沒人照顧，會不會有些時候覺得害怕呢？」

玫瑰說：「花圃中間有棵樹，它不照顧我們的話，還有什麼用處？」

愛麗絲問：「但如果發生危險，它可以做什麼？」

玫瑰說：「它會汪叫。」

一朵雛菊大喊：「它會像狗一樣汪汪叫，那就是為什麼它的樹枝會被稱作樹枝！」

另一朵雛菊高聲說：「你連這個都不知道？」這時全部的雛菊開始一起大喊，空氣中似乎充滿小小的尖叫聲。虎皮百合大喊：「安靜！每朵都給我閉嘴！」它激烈地搖來晃去，氣得全身發抖，「她們知道我抓不到她們！」它氣

喘吁吁，顫抖的頭彎向愛麗絲，「否則絕對不敢這樣！」

愛麗絲用安撫的語氣說：「別介意！」她彎下腰，對著再度開始吵鬧不休的雛菊低聲說：「如果你們再不閉嘴，我就把你們都摘下來！」

雛菊立刻安靜下來，好幾朵粉紅雛菊嚇得發白。

虎皮百合說：「這就對了！這些雛菊最壞了，如果其中一朵說話，每一朵都開始嘰嘰喳喳，光聽她們吵鬧就足以讓人枯萎！」

愛麗絲說：「為什麼你們這麼會說話呢？」愛麗絲希望讚美的話可以讓虎皮百合心情變好一點，「我去過很多花園，但沒有一朵花兒會說話。」

虎皮百合說：「你伸手往下摸摸土壤，就會明白。」

愛麗絲摸了摸土，說道：「土壤很硬，但我不懂這跟花兒會不會講話有什麼關係。」

虎皮百合說：「大部分花園的花圃都太軟了，所以花兒總是在睡覺。」

這聽起來很有道理，愛麗絲很高興地學到這一點，她說：「我以前從來沒

想過！」

玫瑰花相當苛刻地說：「依我看來，你根本不曾思考。」

紫羅蘭忽然開口：「我沒看過比你更笨的人。」愛麗絲嚇得跳起來，因為它剛剛一直沒開口。

虎皮百合大喊：「閉上你的嘴！你說得好像看過別人似的！你都把頭藏在葉子下面，打鼾度過時間，直到最後都像個花苞一樣，對這個世界上的事一無所知！」

愛麗絲說：「這座花園裡除了我以外，還有別人嗎？」她決定不理會玫瑰的評語。

玫瑰說：「花園裡還有另一朵花，像你一樣會走來走去。我覺得很奇怪，你們怎麼會走路（虎百合說：「你什麼都覺得奇怪！」），不過她長得比你還茂盛。」

愛麗絲急切地問：「她跟我很像嗎？」因為她想到：「花園的某個地方有

「另一位小女孩！」

玫瑰說：「嗯，她長得跟你一樣笨拙，不過，她的顏色比你紅……花瓣比你短。」

虎皮百合說：「她的花瓣整齊密匝，就像大麗花，不像你的花瓣一樣亂七八糟的。」

玫瑰花好心地補上一句：「但那不是你的錯，你知道吧，你開始凋謝了，花瓣難免會有點不整齊。」

愛麗絲非常不喜歡這個說法，所以換個話題問：「她來過這裡嗎？」

玫瑰說：「我敢說，你很快就會看到她了，她是有九根尖刺的那種，你知道吧？」

愛麗絲略感好奇地問：「她的尖刺戴在哪裡？」

玫瑰回答：「當然是戴在頭上啊，我剛剛還覺得奇怪，你怎麼沒有尖刺，我還以為你們都有。」

飛燕草大喊：「她來了！我聽到她的腳步聲了，蹬！蹬！她沿著碎石子路走過來了！」

愛麗絲急忙東張西望，發現那是紅棋王后來了。愛麗絲一看到她就說：「她長大了許多！」確實如此，愛麗絲第一次在壁爐灰燼裡發現紅棋王后的時候，她只有八公分高，而現在的她比愛麗絲高出半個頭！

玫瑰說：「那是因為空氣新鮮的緣故，這裡的空氣清新美妙極了！」

愛麗絲說：「我過去跟她見個面。」雖然這些花兒很有趣，但她覺得跟一位真正的王后說話更是了不起。

玫瑰說：「那樣走的話，你絕不可能見到她，我勸你朝著反方向走。」

愛麗絲覺得這聽起來沒道理，所以不吭聲，但立刻邁步走向紅棋王后。愛麗絲吃了一驚，因為紅棋王后瞬間就不見蹤影，而且愛麗絲發現自己又回到房子的大門前。

愛麗絲有點生氣，她退了回去，四處尋找紅棋王后（最後她終於辨認出王

后在遙遠的地方），愛麗
絲心想，這次試著往反方
向走吧。

這次順利成功了！
愛麗絲才走不到一分
鐘，就發現自己與紅棋王
后面對面，而且剛才她一
直想爬上去的小山也出現
在眼前。

紅棋王后說：「你從
哪裡來的？你要去哪裡？
抬起頭來，好好說話，別
一直玩手指頭。」

愛麗絲乖乖照做，並盡可能好好解釋她找不到自己的路。

紅棋王后說：「我不懂你說『自己的路』是什麼意思，這裡所有的路都屬於我，不過你到底為什麼會來這裡？」她用和藹一點的語氣補了一句：「你可以一邊思考要說什麼，一邊行屈膝禮，這樣可以節省時間。」

愛麗絲覺得這樣有點奇怪，但她非常敬畏王后，不敢質疑她。她心想：「我回家後試試看，下次晚餐遲到的時候，我就行個屈膝禮。」

紅棋王后邊看手錶邊說：「現在你該回答了！講話時嘴巴張大一點，而且每次都要加上『陛下』。」

「我只是想看看花園是什麼模樣，陛下……」

紅棋王后說：「這就對了。」她拍拍愛麗絲的頭，愛麗絲根本不喜歡王后這麼做，「不過，你說到『花園』嘛，與我看過的花園相比，這個花園簡直是荒地。」

愛麗絲不敢與她爭論這一點，只能繼續說：「而且我想找一條路到那座小

山的山頂……」

紅棋王后打斷她：「你說到『山頂』，我可以帶你看看真正的小山，相比之下，這座只能稱為山谷。」

愛麗絲說：「不，我不可能那樣說……」她太驚訝了，最終還是對王后頂嘴，「您知道，山丘不可能是山谷。」

紅棋王后搖搖頭，「你說那是胡說八道，那是胡說八道……」

愛麗絲再度行個屈膝禮，因為紅棋王后的語氣聽起來好像有點生氣。她們默默走著，直到來到山頂。

愛麗絲默默站著，好幾分鐘都沒說話，放眼四望整片田野。這片田野真奇特！許多小溪筆直地從一端流到另一端，小溪之間的土地被一排排綠色小樹籬隔成方格。

愛麗絲終於開口：「天啊，這片原野隔得像一片巨大的棋盤！」她開心地

補充說：「上面應該有些棋子四處走動……真的有！」她開始興奮地心跳加速，繼續說：「這是正在下的一盤超大西洋棋啊……這個棋盤跟世界一樣大……如果這片田野算是世界的話。喔，真有趣啊！我真希望我也是其中一個棋子！如果我能加入，當個士兵也沒關係……不過，我最想當的當然是王后。」

愛麗絲說這句話時，很害羞地看了真正的王后一眼，但紅棋王后只是和氣微笑著說：「這很容易辦到，你喜歡的話，可以當白棋王后的士兵，

因為莉莉年紀太小了，還不能參加遊戲。你從第二格開始走，走到第八格就可以變成王后了。」就在這時，不知怎的，她們開始跑了起來。

愛麗絲後來回想，始終弄不清當時她們怎麼開始的，只記得她們手牽著手奔跑，紅棋王后跑得極快，愛麗絲只能努力跟上。然而，紅棋王后一直高喊：「快一點！快一點！」但愛麗絲覺得沒辦法跑得更快了，不過她根本喘不過氣來講這件事。

整件事最奇怪的地方是她們身邊的樹木與其他景物絲毫不動，無論她們跑得多快，卻好像始終沒超越任何東西。可憐的愛麗絲很困惑，她心想：「我懷疑是不是所有的東西都跟著我們一起移動？」紅棋王后似乎猜中她的想法，因為她大喊：「快一點！別想說話！」

愛麗絲根本不想說話，她覺得自己上氣不接下氣，彷彿從此再也無法說話了。但紅棋王后還是不斷大喊：「快一點！快一點！」她拉著愛麗絲跑，愛麗絲最後氣喘吁吁地問：「我們快到了嗎？」

紅棋王后回答：「什麼『快到了嗎』！十分鐘前就已經跑過頭啦！快一點！」她們繼續默默跑了一陣子，風兒在愛麗絲的耳邊呼嘯而過，她覺得頭髮都快被風吹走了。

紅棋王后大喊：「好！好！快一點！快一點！」她們跑得極快，最後簡直就像飛掠過空中，幾乎足不沾地。忽然間，就在愛麗絲快要筋疲力竭的時候，她們停了下來，愛麗絲癱坐在地，氣喘吁吁，頭暈眼花。

紅棋王后扶起愛麗絲，讓她靠著一棵樹，接著和藹地說：「現在你可以休

息一會兒了。」

愛麗絲環顧四周，非常吃驚，「哎呀，我想我們剛剛一直在這棵樹下！一切都沒變！」

紅棋王后說：「當然呀，不然你以為是怎麼樣？」

愛麗絲說：「嗯，在我們那邊的國度……」她還是有點喘，「如果像我們剛才那樣跑得很快，又跑了很久，通常都會跑到別的地方。」

紅棋王后說：「真是個慢吞吞的國度！你看，在我們這裡，你得用盡全力拚命跑，才能停在原地，如果想到別的地方，至少得跑兩倍快！」

愛麗絲說：「拜託，我寧可不去，我待在這裡就心滿意足了……可是我好熱又好渴！」

紅棋王后和善地說：「我知道你想要什麼！」她從口袋裡掏出一個小盒子，「吃片餅乾吧？」

雖然餅乾根本不是愛麗絲想要的，但她覺得拒絕很失禮，所以接過餅乾，

努力吃下去。餅乾非常乾，她心想這輩子從沒像這樣差點給噎死。

紅棋王后說：「趁你吃餅乾休息的時候，我來量一下。」她從口袋裡拿出標好尺度的一條緞帶，開始量起地面，並在這裡與那裡插上小木樁。

「我走到兩百公分的地方，」紅棋王后一邊說，一邊插入木樁標示距離，「我會指引你方向，再吃一片餅乾吧？」

愛麗絲說：「不，謝謝，一片就非常夠了！」

紅棋王后說：「我想你解渴了吧？」

愛麗絲不知道如何回答，但幸好紅棋王后並沒等她回答，而是繼續往下說：「我走到三百公分的地方，會再說一次，免得你忘了。我走到四百公分的地方，就要跟你說再見了。我走到五百公分的地方，就要走了！」

此時，紅棋王后已經插好全部的木樁，愛麗絲興味盎然地看著王后走回樹下，然後開始沿著那排木樁慢慢往前走。

王后走到兩百公分處的木樁時，回過頭說：「你知道吧，士兵第一步可以

走兩格，所以你要非常迅速地通過第三格……我想你就搭火車吧。你會發現立刻就到了第四格，嗯，那格屬於崔德頓與崔德迪。第五格幾乎都是水，第六格屬於蛋頭先生……你怎麼都沒有意見？」

愛麗絲結結巴巴：「我……剛剛……我不知道我需要發表意見……。」

紅棋王后繼續用嚴厲的責備語氣說：「你剛剛應該說：『非常感謝您的指點。』不過我們就當作你說過了。第七格全是森林，不過會有一名騎士為你帶路。到了第八格，我們就可以一起當王后，那時可以大吃大喝，痛快玩樂！」

愛麗絲起身行個屈膝禮，然後再度坐下來。

紅棋王后走到下一個木樁，再度回頭說：「如果你想不出有些東西的英文怎麼說，就用法文說吧。走路時腳尖朝外，還要記住你的身分！」這次王后沒等愛麗絲行屈膝禮，就快步走到下一個木樁，她轉頭稍停，說聲「再見」，接著急急忙忙走向最後一個木樁。

愛麗絲始終不清楚這是怎麼發生的，但紅棋王后一走到最後一個木樁，就

消失無蹤。王后究竟是消失在空氣中？還是飛快跑進森林裡？（愛麗絲心想：「王后真的可以跑得超快！」）實在猜不出來。不過，王后不見了，愛麗絲想起自己是個士兵，很快就輪到她走下一步了。

你覺得我們現在待的世界是「跑得很快，又跑了很久，就可以跑到別的地方」，還是「用盡全力拼命跑，才能停在原地，如果想到別的地方，至少得跑兩倍快」？

第三章　鏡中昆蟲

當然，愛麗絲要做的第一件事就是好好觀察她即將遊歷的這個國度。愛麗絲踮起腳尖，希望能看得更遠一些，她心想：「這好像在上地理課，主要河川……沒有；主要山嶽：我就站在唯一的山上，但我想這座山應該沒有名字；主要城鎮：咦，那邊在採花蜜的是什麼生物？不可能是蜜蜂……從來沒有人能看見一點五公里外的蜜蜂……」她靜靜站了一會兒，看著其中一隻在花叢裡穿梭忙碌，牠把吸管伸進花朵裡，愛麗絲心想：「就像普通蜜蜂一樣。」

但那根本不是一隻蜜蜂，事實上，那是一隻大象，愛麗絲很快就看出來了，不過一開始她嚇得喘不過氣。她接著想：「那些花一定很大！那些花就像拆掉屋頂的小屋，把花莖伸進去……裡面一定產出很多花蜜！我要下去看

看。」愛麗絲開始跑下山，突然又停下腳步，「不行，現在還不能去。」她試著為自己忽然變得畏縮找藉口。「穿梭在大象群裡，若沒有一根長長的樹枝把牠們撥開，那可不行。如果有人問我覺得在裡面散步是什麼感覺，那就太好玩了，我會說：『還不錯囉——（這時她的頭輕輕一甩，這是她最愛做的姿勢）只是天氣太熱，灰塵很多，而且那些大象還很會捉弄人！』」

停頓片刻，愛麗絲又說：「我想還是走另一條路下山好了，或許以後再去看大象，而且我真的很想到第三格！」

所以愛麗絲有了這個藉口，就跑下山，跳過六條小溪中的第一條。

列車長把頭伸進車窗說：「請出示車票！」大家立刻掏出車票，車票跟人一樣大，整個車廂好像塞滿了。

列車長繼續說：「好了！孩子，拿出你的車票！」他惱怒地看著愛麗絲，許多人異口同聲地說（愛麗絲心想：「就跟合唱一樣」）：「孩子莫讓他等待！一分鐘值一千萬！」

愛麗絲害怕地說：「對不起，我沒有票，我上車的地方沒有售票處。」那片合聲再次響起：「無地可設售票處，一吋地值一千萬！」

列車長說：「別找藉口了，你應該向火車司機買票！」那片合聲再度響起：「火車司機開火車，一股噴煙一千萬！」

愛麗絲心想：「說什麼都沒用。」這次由於她沒說話，那片合聲也就沒響起，但她很驚訝地發現，大家竟然齊聲在想（我希望你們了解「齊聲在想」是什麼意思，因為我必須承認我不懂）：「最好什麼也別說，一言值一千萬！」

愛麗絲心想：「今晚我一定會夢到一千萬，我知道一定會！」。

整個過程當中，列車長一直在觀察愛麗絲……起初用望遠鏡，接著用顯微鏡，最後用觀劇的望遠鏡。最後他說：「你搭錯方向了。」就關上窗走了。

坐在愛麗絲對面的一位紳士（穿著白紙做的衣服）說：「這麼小的孩子，即使不知道自己的名字，也應該知道要往哪個方向！」

坐在白衣紳士旁邊的山羊閉著眼睛大聲說：「就算她不認得字母，也應該

知道前往售票處的路！」

坐在山羊旁邊的是一隻甲蟲（這個車廂坐滿古怪的乘客），他們好像得照規矩輪流說些話，所以甲蟲接著說：「應該把她當成行李送回去！」

愛麗絲看不到甲蟲旁邊坐的是誰，但一道嘶啞的聲音接著說：「換火車頭……」此時那道聲音嗆住了，不得不閉嘴。

愛麗絲心想：「那聽起來像一匹馬。」這時一道非常微弱的聲音在她耳邊說：「你可以用『馬嘶』和『嘶啞』編個笑話。」

接著，遠遠一道溫和的聲音說：「一定要給她貼上『內有女孩，小心輕放』的標籤……」

之後許多道聲音繼續說（愛麗絲心想：「這個車廂裡的乘客真多！」）：「她有頭，應該郵寄回去……」、「應該用電報送回去……」、「應該叫她拉著火車走完剩下的路……」

但是穿著白紙衣服的那位紳士彎身在愛麗絲耳邊低語：「親愛的，別在意他們說的話。但每次火車停下來，你都要買一張來回票。」

愛麗絲頗不耐煩地說：「我才不要！我根本就不該搭這班火車！我剛才還在森林裡……真希望我能回到那裡！」

那道微弱的聲音在愛麗絲耳邊響起：「你可以用『事竟成就有心做』編個笑話。」

愛麗絲說：「別鬧了！」她東張西望，想看看那道聲音來自哪裡，卻徒勞無功，「如果你這麼想叫別人說笑話，為什麼自己不編一個？」

那道微弱的聲音深深地嘆了一口氣，顯然非常悶悶不樂。愛麗絲本來想說些同情的話來安慰它，她心想：「如果這嘆氣聲像別人一樣大聲就好了。」但這個嘆息聲非常微弱，若不是緊貼在她耳邊，她根本聽不到，結果這搔得她的耳朵很癢，所以她分心了，無法認真關心這個不快樂的可憐小東西。

那道微弱的聲音繼續說：「我知道你是朋友，你是親愛的朋友，也是老朋友。雖然我是昆蟲，但你不會傷害我。」

愛麗絲有點急切地問：「哪一種昆蟲？」她真正想問的是牠會不會叮人，但她覺得這個問題頗失禮。

「什麼？所以你不……」那道微弱的聲音才剛響起，就被火車引擎的尖銳聲音掩蓋了，大家都嚇得跳了起來，愛麗絲也是。

那匹馬把頭伸出窗外，又靜靜縮回來說：「只不過是一條小溪，我們得跳過去。」大家似乎都很滿意這個答案，但愛麗絲想到火車竟然會跳，不禁有點緊張。她自言自語：「不過，這會帶我們到第四格，算是令人安慰！」片刻

後，她感覺整節車廂筆直飛到空中，她嚇得一把抓住離她最近的東西，碰巧抓到山羊的鬍子。

但是愛麗絲一碰到山羊的鬍子，鬍子彷彿就融化了，接著她發現自己靜靜坐在一棵樹下，那隻蚊子（就是剛剛跟她聊天的昆蟲）穩穩停在她頭頂上的小樹枝上，正在用翅膀為她搧風。

這無疑是一隻非常大的蚊子，愛麗絲心想：「牠跟雞一樣大！」但她不緊張，因為他們已經聊了很久。

蚊子把剛剛講到一半的話說完：「所以你不是全部的昆蟲都喜歡？」牠的語氣平靜，彷彿剛剛沒發生任何事。

愛麗絲說：「我喜歡會說話的昆蟲。我那邊的昆蟲都不會說話。」

蚊子問：「你那邊的昆蟲裡，你喜歡哪一種？」

愛麗絲解釋：「我根本不喜歡昆蟲，因為我很怕昆蟲，至少怕那些大隻的昆蟲，但我可以把一些昆蟲的名字告訴你。」

蚊子漫不經心地說：「如果叫牠們的名字，牠們肯定會回應吧？」

「我從來都不知道牠們會回應。」

蚊子說：「如果牠們不會回應，那牠們有名字又有什麼用呢？」

愛麗絲說：「對牠們沒用，但我想對幫牠們取名字的人有用吧，不然為什麼所有東西都有名字呢？」

蚊子回答：「我不知道。前面那座森林裡的所有東西都沒有名字。不管怎樣，繼續說你那邊的昆蟲名字吧，別浪費時間。」

愛麗絲開口：「嗯，我們那邊有馬蠅。」她扳著手指，數著昆蟲名字。

蚊子說：「好，那邊有一棵灌木，如果你仔細看，就會看到枝葉上面有隻搖搖馬蠅，牠整隻都是木頭做的，從一根樹枝搖到另一根樹枝，四處移動。」

愛麗絲非常好奇地問：「牠吃什麼呢？」

蚊子說：「樹汁與鋸木屑。」

愛麗絲興致盎然地盯著那隻搖搖馬蠅，她判斷牠才剛剛刷上新漆，看起來非常鮮豔，而且黏呼呼的。她接著往下數。

「我們那邊還有蜻蜓。」

蚊子說：「看看你頭上的那根樹枝，那裡有一隻噴火蜻蜓，牠的身體是葡萄乾布丁，翅膀是冬青葉，頭是浸了白蘭地的燃燒葡萄乾。」

愛麗絲問了一樣的問題：「牠吃什麼呢？」

蚊子回答：「牛奶燕麥粥與水果碎肉餡餅，牠就住在耶誕禮盒裡。」

愛麗絲仔細端詳那隻頭上著火的噴火蜻蜓，她心想：「我很好奇這是不是昆蟲喜歡飛向燭火的原因……

因為牠們想變成噴火蜻蜓！」愛麗絲接著又說：

「我們那邊還有蝴蝶。」

蚊子說：「目前在你腳邊爬的（愛麗絲嚇得趕緊縮腳），就是一隻奶油麵包蝶，牠的翅膀是塗了奶油的薄片麵包，身體是麵包皮，頭是方糖。」

「牠吃什麼呢？」

「奶油淡茶。」

愛麗絲想到新難題，她說：「萬一牠找不到奶油淡茶，該怎麼辦？」

「那牠當然就死了。」

蚊子說：「這種事不斷發生。」

愛麗絲若有所思地說：「但那種情況一定經常發生吧。」

愛麗絲沉思了一兩分鐘，一言不發，這時蚊子在她頭上嗡嗡地飛來繞去，

自得其樂。最後蚊子又停下來說：「我猜，你不想丟掉名字吧？」

愛麗絲有點不安地說：「當然不想。」

蚊子漫不經心地繼續說：「可是我不明白，想想看如果你回家的時候沒有名字，那有多方便！比方說，家庭女教師想叫你上課，她大喊：『快來──』然後就喊不下去了，因為你沒有名字讓她叫，你當然就不必上課了。」

愛麗絲說：「我敢說那絕對行不通，家庭女教師絕對不會因為這樣就放過我。如果她忘了我的名字，她就會跟其他僕人一樣叫我『小姐』。」

蚊子說：「好，如果她叫你『小姐』，但又沒再說別的，那你當然就可以錯過課程囉。這是個笑話，我希望你講這個笑話。」

愛麗絲問：「為什麼你希望我講這個笑話？這個笑話很爛耶。」

蚊子卻只是深深嘆氣，兩滴豆大的淚珠滑落臉頰。

愛麗絲說：「如果說笑話讓你這麼難過，你就不該再說笑話了。」

蚊子又發出憂鬱的微弱嘆息，這次真的就像把自己嘆得消失了，因為愛麗

絲抬頭看的時候，樹枝上面已經空無一物。愛麗絲靜靜坐了很久，覺得越來越冷，就起身繼續往前走。

不久她來到一片空曠的田野，田野的另一邊是一座森林，看起來比上次的森林陰暗多了。愛麗絲有點害怕，不敢進去，但轉念一想就決定繼續往前走，她心想：「因為我當然不會往回走。」這是前往第八格的唯一道路。

愛麗絲若有所思地自言自語：「這想必就是所有東西都沒有名字的那座森林。我真想知道走進去之後，我的名字會怎麼樣呢？我根本不想丟掉名字，因為這樣他們就得為我取另一個名字，新名字一定很難聽。但我要試著找出撿到我舊名字的生物，多好玩啊！那就像報紙上的尋狗啟事：叫牠『戴許』會回應，脖子戴著銅項圈。想想看，遇到什麼東西都叫叫看『愛麗絲』，直到有回應！不過如果他們聰明的話，根本就不會回應。」

愛麗絲一邊說個不停，一邊漫步走到森林邊，森林看起來非常陰涼。她走進森林裡時自言自語：「嗯，不管怎樣，現在非常舒服，剛剛好熱啊，走進這

個……走進這個……走進這個什麼?」她很驚訝自己居然想不起來那個詞,「我的意思是說走進這個……走進這個……走進這個,反正你知道的!」她伸手摸著樹幹,「我真想知道它怎麼稱呼自己?我想它沒有名字,哎呀,一定沒有名字!」

愛麗絲靜靜站著思考了一會兒,又忽然再度開口:「這件事竟然真的發生了!那麼我是誰?我下定決心要想起來!」但下定決心也沒用,她苦思很久之後,只說得出:「ㄞ,我知道我的名字是ㄞ開頭的!」

這時一隻小鹿漫步過來,牠用溫柔的大眼睛望著愛麗絲,看起來一點也不害怕。愛麗絲說:「過來!過來!」她伸手想摸小鹿,牠卻只是稍微退後,又站住望著她。

小鹿終於開口:「你叫什麼名字?」牠的聲音真是輕柔甜美!

可憐的愛麗絲心想:「我真希望自己知道啊!」她很哀傷地回答:「我現在沒有名字!」

小鹿說：「再想一想，沒有名字不行！」

愛麗絲想了又想，但什麼也想不起來。她膽怯地說：「拜託，可以跟我說你叫什麼名字嗎？那或許能幫我想起自己的名字。」

小鹿說：「如果再往前走一小段路，我就可以告訴你。我在這裡想不起來。」

他們相偕漫步穿越森林，愛麗絲憐愛地摟著小鹿柔軟的脖子，直到走出森

林，來到另一片空曠的田野，這時小鹿忽然一跳，掙脫愛麗絲的摟抱，牠開心地大喊：「我是一隻小鹿！天哪！你是人類的小孩！」小鹿美麗的棕色眼睛閃現驚恐的眼神，牠馬上飛快跑掉。

愛麗絲站在原地看著牠離去，她突然失去親愛的小旅伴，難過得差點哭出來。她說：「不過，我現在知道自己的名字了，也算滿令人安慰。愛麗絲……愛麗絲……我不會再忘記了。現在不知道我該照著哪個路標走呢？」

這個問題不難回答，因為走出森林的路只有一條，兩個路標都指向那條路。愛麗絲自言自語說著：「等到出現岔路，路標指著不同方向的時候，我再決定吧！」

但這樣的情形好像不可能發生。愛麗絲走啊走的，走了好長的路，但每次出現岔路，就一定有兩個路標指向同一條路，一個路標寫著「往崔德頓的家」，另一個路標是「往崔德迪的家」。

愛麗絲最後說：「我想他們一定住在同一間房子！奇怪，我剛剛竟然沒想

到，但我不能在那裡待太久，我登門問候一聲：『你好。』再詢問他們走出森林的路，但願我能在天黑前走到第八格！」愛麗絲繼續漫步前進，邊走邊自言自語，直到拐過一個急轉彎，碰上兩名胖男孩。事出突然，愛麗絲嚇得後退，但很快就恢復鎮定，她確信他們一定就是……

想一想

你喜歡自己的名字嗎？名字對你來說代表了什麼？

第四章　崔德頓和崔德迪

他們站在樹下，各伸出一隻手臂摟著對方的脖子。愛麗絲立刻就分辨出誰是誰，因為一個衣領上繡著「頓」字，另一個繡著「迪」字。她自言自語：「我猜他們的領子後面都有『崔德』兩個字。」

他們兩人站著，一動也不動，愛麗絲差點忘了他們是活人，她正繞到他們的背後，想看看衣領後面究竟有

沒有「崔德」的字樣。這時，衣領繡著「頓」字的男孩忽然開口，嚇了愛麗絲一跳。

他說：「如果你以為我們是蠟像，你就應該付費。你知道，蠟像不是免費給人參觀的，絕對不是！」

衣領繡著「迪」字的男孩補上一句：「反過來說，如果你覺得我們是活人，就應該開口說話。」

「實在很抱歉……」愛麗絲只說得出這句話，因為那首古老童謠的歌詞一直在她腦中響起，就像時鐘滴答滴答的聲音，她忍不住大聲唸出來：

崔德頓與崔德迪，
同意要來打一架。
崔德頓說崔德迪
弄壞新的撥浪鼓。

巨大烏鴉從天降，

黑漆漆就像瀝青。

兩位英雄嚇壞了，

忘了兩人要打架。

崔德頓說：「我知道你在想什麼，但其實不是那樣，絕對不是。」

崔德迪接著說：「反過來說，如果以前是那樣，就可能是那樣，假定現在是那樣，就大概是那樣，但現在不是那樣，就一定不是那樣，這就是邏輯。」

愛麗絲很有禮貌地說：「我在想，哪一條路才可以走出這片森林？天色已經很暗了，該如何走出這座森林？請你們告訴我，好嗎？」

但這兩名胖男孩只是看著對方，咧著嘴笑。

他們看起來簡直就像兩名大塊頭的小學生，愛麗絲忍不住伸手指著崔德頓說：「你先說！」

崔德頓迅速大喊：「絕對不說！」又啪的一聲閉上嘴巴。

愛麗絲又指著崔德迪：「換你說！」但她敢說崔德迪只會大喊「反過來說」，情況也果真如此。

崔德頓說：「嘿，你一開始就錯了！拜訪別人的時候，首先應該要說『你好』然後握手！」此時這對兄弟互摟了一下，接著各自伸出空著的一隻手，想跟愛麗絲握手。

起初愛麗絲怕傷了其中一人的心，所以哪隻手都不願先握。所以，她伸出雙手同時握住他們的手，這是眼前難題的最佳解決辦法，緊接著他們三人就繞著圈圈跳起舞了。（愛麗絲事後回想覺得）這似乎相當自然，甚至她聽到音樂響起也不驚訝，音樂彷彿來自他們頭上的樹，（她勉強聽出）那是樹枝互相摩擦發出的音樂，就像琴弓摩擦提琴一樣。

「但當時真的是很有趣，」（後來愛麗絲把這個故事告訴姐姐），「我發現自己居然在唱《我們圍著桑樹叢轉圈》，也不知道什麼時候開始唱的，但我

覺得好像唱了很久！」

另外兩位舞者很胖，很快就跳得喘不過氣來，崔德頓氣喘吁吁地說：「一首跳個四圈就夠了……」他們頓時停下來，就跟開始跳一樣突然，音樂也同時停了。

接著，他們放開愛麗絲的手，站著默默打量她一會兒。這個情況很尷尬，愛麗絲不知道如何主動開口跟剛剛一起跳舞的人聊天，她自言自語：「現在說『你好』絕對行不通，我們似乎已經認識彼此，不算陌生人了！」

她終於擠出一句：「我想你們不會太累吧？」

崔德頓說：「絕對不會，非常謝謝你的關心。」

崔德迪補上一句：「非常感激。你喜歡詩嗎？」

愛麗絲遲疑地說：「喜……喜歡，很喜歡某些詩。請你們告訴我怎麼走出森林好嗎？」

「我該為她朗誦哪一首詩呢？」崔德迪一邊說，一邊用嚴肅的眼神看著崔

德頓，根本不理會愛麗絲的問題。

崔德頓回答：「《海象與木匠》最長。」他熱情地攬了崔德迪一下。

崔德迪立刻開口背：「太陽照耀著……」

此時愛麗絲鼓起勇氣打斷他，她盡可能有禮貌的說：「如果這首詩很長，可不可以請你們先告訴我哪條路……」

崔德迪對她溫和微笑，再度開始朗誦：

太陽照耀著海面，

竭盡全力放光芒，

全力以赴刷海浪，

刷得浪平又燦亮。

此事古怪又異常，

因為此刻已夜半。

黯淡月亮繃著臉，

因為心中氣太陽，

白日既然已結束，

太陽此時應退場。

「如此無禮又粗魯，

壞了我的好興致。」

汪洋大海一片濕，

沙灘一片乾巴巴。

晴空萬里無雲朵，

朗空無雲晴又晴。

頭上尋無飛鳥跡，

飛鳥不來晴空闊。

海象木匠一同來，
手牽手啊並肩行。
痛哭流涕淚難停，
沙灘綿延無止盡，
「若能盡數把沙除，
世界該有多美好！」

七名女僕七拖把，
掃啊掃個大半年，
你看能否掃得完？
海象問啊木匠答，
「我想應該沒辦法。」
說完苦澀眼淚滴。

「牡蠣跟我來散步。」

海象苦苦勤央求，

開開心心散個步，

沿著美麗的海灘。

我們四個一起走，

手牽手啊齊步行。

年邁牡蠣望著牠，

一言不發嘴閉緊，

年邁牡蠣眨眨眼，

搖搖頭啊不答應，

表示已經做決定，

絕不離開牠老家。

四個年輕小牡蠣，
衝上前想尋樂子，
整裝洗臉細打理，
鞋子擦得亮晶晶。
說來這也真古怪，
牡蠣根本沒有腳。

又有四隻跟著來，
後面又再跟四隻，
成群結隊迅速來，
越來越多的牡蠣，
跳出浪花泡沫中，
爭先恐後爬上岸。

海象木匠帶頭走，

總共走了一里多，

選個石頭歇歇腳，

低矮石頭真方便，

小小牡蠣全站著，

乖乖等候排排站。

海象率先開話匣，

天南地北聊一聊，

鞋子船舶與封蠟，

卷心菜以及國王，

海洋為何熱燙燙，

豬兒是否有翅膀。

牡蠣大聲喊暫停，

聊天暫且先緩緩，

我們身材肥嘟嘟，

全都走得喘吁吁！

木匠安慰說別急，

牡蠣心中好感激。

海象要一條麵包，

麵包絕對不可少，

還要胡椒與好醋，

美味大餐在眼前，

親愛牡蠣請準備，

我們就要享用了。

牡蠣臉色轉鐵青，

大喊口下請留情，

親切和藹待我們，

這番結局太悲悽。

海象稱讚夜色美，

諸位何不賞風景？

感謝你們來此地，

各位真是太美好，

木匠沒有多說話，

「再切一片土司來，

希望你啊別裝聾，

我已經得說兩遍。」

海象坦承很羞愧，
施展詭計欺牡蠣，
帶牠們離鄉背井，
還讓牠們快步走，
「奶油抹得太厚了！」
木匠沒有多說話，

海象哭得淚汪汪，
表達同情與憐憫，
涕淚俱下多哀戚，
挑出最大顆牡蠣，
掏出手帕蓋住臉，
擦拭淚濕的雙眼。

木匠終於說話了，

「牡蠣玩得真開心，準備打道回府囉？」

牡蠣沉默無回應，

其實根本不奇怪，

牠們早被吃光光。

愛麗絲說：「我比較喜歡海象，因為牠有點同情可憐的小牡蠣。」

崔德迪說：「但牠吃得比木匠多，你看牠用手帕蓋住臉，這樣一來，木匠就沒辦法數牠到底吃了幾隻牡蠣，反過來說。」

愛麗絲氣憤地說：「眞卑鄙！那麼我比較喜歡木匠……如果他吃的牡蠣沒有海象那麼多的話。」

崔德頓說：「但他是能吃多少就吃多少。」

這真是難題，愛麗絲沉默一會兒後，才又開口：「哼！他們兩個都是討厭鬼……」此時她說到一半就嚇得停住了，因為她聽見附近的森林裡傳來某種聲音，聽起來就像大型蒸氣引擎在噴氣。但愛麗絲更擔心那可能是野獸，她膽怯地問：「這附近有獅子或老虎嗎？」

崔德迪說：「那只是紅棋國王在打鼾。」

這對兄弟大喊：「我們去看看他！」他們一人牽起愛麗絲的一隻手，帶領她到紅棋國王睡覺的地方。

崔德頓說：「他的睡相可愛吧？」

老實說，愛麗絲並不覺得可愛，紅棋國王戴著高聳的紅色睡帽，帽尖綴有流蘇，躺著縮成一團，睡相邋遢，大聲打鼾……崔德頓說：

「打鼾打得這麼大聲，頭都要掉了！」

愛麗絲說：「我怕他這樣睡在濕濕的草地上會感冒。」她是個非常體貼的小女孩。

崔德迪說：「他正在做夢，你覺得他夢到什麼？」

愛麗絲說：「誰也猜不到吧。」

崔德迪得意洋洋地拍手大喊：「哈，夢到了你呀！如果他沒夢到你，你猜你會在哪裡？」

愛麗絲說：「當然就在現在這裡啊。」

崔德迪輕蔑地反駁：「才不是！你哪裡都不在！哈，你只是他夢裡的東西而已！」

崔德頓補充說：「如果紅棋國王醒了，你就會消失……呼！就像蠟燭熄滅那樣！」

愛麗絲氣憤地說：「才不會！還有，如果我只是他夢裡的東西，我倒想知道，那你們是什麼呢？」

崔德頓說：「跟你一樣！」

崔德迪大聲說：「跟你一樣！跟你一樣！」

他喊得很大聲，愛麗絲忍不住說：「噓！你那麼吵，我怕你會把他吵醒！」

崔德頓說：「嗯，你怕吵醒他也沒用，你只是他夢裡的東西而已。你很清楚你根本不是真的。」

愛麗絲說：「我是真的！」她哭了起來。

崔德迪說：「你哭也不會變得真一點，而且沒什麼好哭的。」

愛麗絲說：「如果我不是真的，」她半哭半笑，這一切似乎太過荒謬，

「我應該不會哭啊。」

崔德頓以非常輕蔑的語氣插嘴：「你該不會以為那些是真的眼淚吧？」

愛麗絲心想：「我知道他們是胡說八道，為了這個哭實在太傻了。」因此她擦掉眼淚，盡可能開朗地繼續說：「不管怎樣，我最好趕快離開森林，因為天色已經很黑了。你們覺得會下雨嗎？」

崔德頓打開一把大傘，罩住自己與崔德迪，再抬頭看著傘說：「不會，我覺得不會下雨，至少……這把傘下面不會，絕對不會。」

崔德迪說：「嗯，可能會吧……如果老天想下雨的話，我們並不反對，反過來說。」

「但傘外可能下雨吧？」

愛麗絲心想：「自私鬼！」她正打算說句「晚安」就離開他們，這時崔德頓忽然從傘下跳出來，抓住她的手腕。

他說：「你看到那個了嗎？」他氣得連聲音都哽住了，他的眼睛立刻變得又大又黃，顫抖的手指指著樹下一個白色小東西。

愛麗絲仔細查看那個白色小東西後，說道：「那只是個撥浪鼓而已，又不是響尾蛇。」她以為崔德頓嚇壞了，趕緊補了一句：「那只是舊的撥浪鼓而已，又舊又破爛！」

崔德頓大喊：「我就知道！」他開始瘋狂跺腳，扯著頭髮，「它一定是被

人弄壞的！」他瞪著崔德迪，崔德迪立刻坐在地上，設法躲在傘下。

愛麗絲搭著他的手臂上，以安撫的語氣說：「你沒必要為了舊的撥浪鼓生這麼大的氣。」

崔德頓大吼：「可是那個不是舊的！」他更氣了，「我告訴你，那個是新的……我昨天才買的……我好好的、全新的撥浪鼓！」他的聲音越來越高，變成了尖叫。

這時崔德迪一直設法收傘，想把自己藏在裡面，這個行為非常怪異，這讓愛麗絲的注意力從生氣的崔德頓身上轉

移到崔德迪。但崔德迪沒成功，最後翻滾倒地，身子包在雨傘裡，只有頭露在外面。

他躺在地上，嘴巴與大眼睛一開一闔……愛麗絲心想：「他看起來真像一條魚！」

崔德頓稍微冷靜一點了，他說：「你應該同意打一架吧？」

崔德迪繃著臉回答：「好吧。」他從傘下爬出來，「不過她必須協助我們穿上服裝。」

於是這對兄弟手牽手走進森林裡，很快就抱著一大堆東西回來，像是靠枕、毛毯、壁爐前的地毯、桌巾、餐巾、煤桶。崔德頓說：「你很會別東西與綁東西吧？不管用什麼方法，這裡的東西都必須穿戴上身。」

後來愛麗絲說，她一輩子沒見過那麼手忙腳亂的場面，這對兄弟忙東忙西，把一大堆東西穿戴上身，還麻煩她幫忙綁繩子與扣鈕扣。「說真的，等到他們穿戴完畢，簡直就像兩捆舊衣！」她一邊自言自語，一邊用靠枕圍著崔德

迪的脖子，套句他的話：「這樣腦袋才不會被砍掉。」

崔德迪很嚴肅地補充道：「你懂的，戰鬥時最嚴重的情況，就是腦袋被砍掉。」

愛麗絲大笑出聲，但趕快努力假裝在咳嗽。

崔德頓說：「我的臉色很蒼白嗎？」他走過來，請愛麗絲幫他綁好頭盔。（他稱之為頭盔，但那看起來無疑更像是燉鍋。）

愛麗絲溫和回答：「嗯……對……有一點。」

他低聲繼續說：「我平常很勇敢，只是今天剛好頭痛。」

崔德迪說：「我今天牙齒痛！」他偷聽到崔德頓說的話，「我比你要嚴重多了！」

愛麗絲說：「那我想你們今天最好還是別打了吧。」她覺得這是個講和的好機會。

崔德頓說：「我們必須打一下，但我不想打太久。現在幾點？」

崔德迪看看手錶說：「四點半。」

崔德頓說：「我們打到六點鐘，然後吃晚餐。」

崔德迪憂愁地說：「很好，她可以看我們打，但最好別太靠近。」他補上一句：「我打得起勁的時候，通常是看到什麼就打什麼。」

崔德頓大喊：「我是打得到的東西都打，不管我看不看得見。」

愛麗絲笑出來：「我猜，你們一定經常打到樹木。」

崔德頓露出滿意的微笑，環顧四周，他說：「等到我們打完，我想周圍的

樹木應該都倒了！」

愛麗絲說：「一切就只爲了一個撥浪鼓！」她仍希望讓他們覺得有些羞

愧，竟然爲了這種小事打架。

崔德頓說：「如果那個撥浪鼓不是新的，我才不會那麼在意。」

愛麗絲心想：「我眞希望那隻大烏鴉會來！」

崔德頓對崔德迪說：「你知道的，我們只有一把劍，但你可以用那把雨

傘，它跟劍一樣鋒利。只是我們得趕快開始打，天色很黑了。」

崔德迪說：「越來越黑。」

天色突然黑了，愛麗絲以爲一定是大雷雨來了。她說：「好厚的烏雲！而

且來得眞快！哎呀，我想那它長了翅膀吧！」

崔德頓嚇得尖聲大喊：「烏鴉來了！」這對兄弟拔腿就跑，一下子就不見

蹤影。

愛麗絲跑了一小段路，衝進森林，接著停在一棵大樹下。她心想：「我在

這裡，烏鴉絕對抓不到我，牠太巨大了，擠不進森林裡。但我希望牠別這樣拍翅膀，那在森林裡掀起颶風了……有人的披肩被吹到這裡了！」

想一想

在崔德頓和崔德迪背誦的《海象與木匠》這首詩中，你覺得是海象比較壞還是木匠？為什麼？

第五章　羊毛與水

愛麗絲一邊說，一邊抓住那條披肩，四處張望尋找披肩的主人。不久後，白棋王后穿越森林，瘋狂跑來，兩臂張開，宛如飛翔。愛麗絲拿著披肩，很有禮貌地迎上前。

「我很高興剛好在路上撿到它。」愛麗絲一邊說，一邊幫白棋王后圍上披肩。

白棋王后只是露出無助害怕的表情望著她，不斷重複喃喃說著同一句話，聽起來像是「麵包與奶油、麵包與奶油」。愛麗絲認為如果她要跟王后攀談，一定要自己先開口，因此她怯生生地開口：「很榮幸與您談話，請問您是白棋王后陛下嗎？」

白棋王后說：「嗯，對，如果你要說那是打理服裝的話，不過我完全不這麼認為！」

愛麗絲認為一開始聊天就要爭辯的話，絕對不行，所以她微笑說：「如果陛下願意教我正確的方法，我一定盡力做好。」

可憐的白棋王后咕噥：「但我根本不要別人幫我！剛剛我自己花了兩個鐘頭穿衣服。」

白棋王后的模樣邋邋遢遢不堪，愛麗絲認為如果王后請人幫她打理服裝，她的儀容一定整齊多了。愛麗絲心想：「她身上的每樣東西都歪七扭八，而且全身別滿別針！」於是她大聲對王后說：「請問可以讓我幫您整理披肩嗎？」

王后憂鬱地說：「我不知道這披肩怎麼回事！我想它大概發脾氣了，我拿別針把它別在這裡，又別在那裡，但就是無法讓它開心！」

愛麗絲說：「如果您把別針全部別在同一邊，披肩就沒辦法變得平整。」

她為白棋王后輕輕弄正披肩，「天啊，您的頭髮真亂！」

白棋王后嘆氣
說：「刷子纏在頭髮
裡了！而且我昨天弄
丟梳子了。」

愛麗絲小心翼翼
地取出刷子，再盡力
把白棋王后的頭髮打
理整齊，接著重新整
理王后身上的別針。

愛麗絲說道：「看！
現在您看起來好多
了！我想您真的該有
個貼身侍女！」

白棋王后說：「我很樂意雇用你！週薪兩塊錢，每隔一天供應果醬。」

愛麗絲忍不住笑出來，她說：「我不需要您雇用我……而且，我不喜歡吃果醬。」

白棋王后說：「那可是上好的果醬喔！」

「呃，謝謝，不管怎樣，今天我不想吃果醬。」

王后說：「今天就算你想吃也吃不到。規矩是明天有果醬，昨天有果醬，但今天永遠沒有果醬。」

愛麗絲反駁：「有時一定可以吃到『今天的果醬』吧？」

白棋王后說：「不，不可能。每隔一天供應果醬，今天可不是『每隔一天』，你懂的。」

愛麗絲說：「我不懂，這讓人非常困惑！」

白棋王后和藹地說：「這就是過著時光倒流生活的結果，一開始總是讓人有點頭暈眼花……」

愛麗絲很驚訝地說：「過著時光倒流的生活！我從來沒聽過這種事！」

「……但這樣有個很大的好處，那就是記憶會有兩個方向。」

愛麗絲說：「我很確定我的記憶只有一個方向，我不可能記得還沒發生的事情。」

白棋王后說：「只有過去的記憶是很差的記憶。」

愛麗絲鼓起勇氣問：「敢問王后陛下，您記得最清楚的是哪種事呢？」

白棋王后漫不經心地回答：「噢，就是下下星期發生的事。」她一邊把一大塊藥布貼在手指上，一邊繼續說：「比如說，國王的信差目前被關在牢裡受罰，但是下星期三才會受審，當然啦，審判後他才會犯罪。」

愛麗絲說：「假如他根本沒犯罪呢？」

「那樣就更好了，不是嗎？」白棋王后一邊說，一邊用緞帶綁住手指上的藥布。

愛麗絲覺得她無法反駁這個說法，她說：「那樣當然更好，但他受了處

罰，那可不算更好。」

白棋王后說：「無論如何，這點你就錯了。你受過處罰嗎？」

愛麗絲說：「只有做錯事的時候。」

白棋王后得意洋洋地說：「你受了處罰一定變得更好，我知道的！」

愛麗絲說：「對，可是，我是先做錯事情，之後才受到處罰，這完全是兩回事。」

白棋王后說：「如果你沒有做錯事，那就更好了，更好，更好，更好！」她每說一次「更好」，聲音就變得更加尖銳，到了最後根本是尖叫。

愛麗絲正要開口：「這一定有不對的地方……」這時白棋王后開始大聲尖叫，愛麗絲不得不中斷。王后高喊：「噢，噢，噢！」她甩著手，彷彿想要將手甩掉，「我的手指流血了！噢，噢，噢！」

白棋王后的尖叫聲簡直就像蒸汽火車引擎的汽笛聲，愛麗絲不得不用手摀住耳朵。

等到白棋王后停止尖叫，愛麗絲立刻抓緊機會說：「到底是怎麼回事？您刺傷手指了？」

白棋王后說：「還沒刺傷，但快了……噢，噢，噢！」

愛麗絲很想笑，她問：「您預計什麼時候會刺傷呢？」

可憐的白棋王后呻吟著說：「我把披肩重新固定好的時候，胸針就直接鬆開。噢，噢！」她說這些話的時候，胸針果然彈開了，王后伸手亂抓，想把胸針重新扣好。

愛麗絲大喊：「小心！您抓歪了！」愛麗絲想抓住胸針，但為時已晚，胸針一滑，刺傷了白棋王后的手指。

白棋王后微笑對愛麗絲說：「你看，這就是我流血的原因，現在你明白這裡事情發生的順序了吧。」

愛麗絲問：「那為什麼現在不尖叫了呢？」愛麗絲舉起雙手，準備再次搗住耳朵。

白棋王后說：「喔，我剛剛已經尖叫過了，為什麼要再尖叫一次？」

這時，天色漸漸轉亮。愛麗絲說：「我想那隻大烏鴉一定飛走了，真高興牠走了，剛剛我還以為天黑了呢。」

白棋王后說：「我真希望自己高興得起來！但我總是記不住規則。你住在這座森林裡一定很快樂吧，隨時想開心就能開心！」

愛麗絲憂鬱地說：「可是在這裡很寂寞！」愛麗絲一想到自己多麼寂寞，兩顆豆大的淚珠就滾落臉頰。

可憐的白棋王后絕望地扭著雙手，大聲說：「噢！別這樣。想想看，你多棒啊；想想看，你今天走了好長的路；想想看，現在幾點鐘了。想想任何事都行，就是別哭！」

愛麗絲聽了就忍不住笑出來，儘管仍淚眼汪汪。她問：「想著別的事情就不會哭了嗎？」

白棋王后非常果斷地說：「事情就是這樣。誰都無法同時做兩件事，你懂

的。首先想想你的年紀⋯⋯你幾歲了？」

「正好七歲半。」

「你不必說『正好』，你不說我也相信你。現在我要說一件事讓你相信看看，我才一百零一歲五個月又一天。」

愛麗絲說：「我不相信這件事！」

白棋王后同情地說：「你不相信？再試一次，深呼吸，閉上眼睛。」

愛麗絲笑了出來，她說：「試也沒用，人們無法相信不可能的事情！」

白棋王后說：「我敢說你練習得不多，我跟你一樣大的時候，每天總要練習半小時。唔，有時我在早餐之前就能相信六件不可能的事情。我的披肩又飛走啦！」

白棋王后說話時，胸針又彈開了，一陣強風忽然吹來，把披風吹過小溪。

王后再度張開雙臂，飛快地追著披風，這次她自己抓住了披風。她得意洋洋地大喊：「我抓到了！現在你看，我把披肩別好了，我自己別的！」

愛麗絲隨著白棋王后越過小溪，彬彬有禮地說：「那麼我想您的手指現在好些了吧？」

白棋王后大喊：「噢，好多了！」她繼續大喊，聲音越來越高，變成了尖叫；「好多了！好……了！好……多……了！好……多……咩！」最後一個字的尾音變成拉得很長的咩咩聲，簡直就像羊叫聲，愛麗絲吃了一驚。

她看著白棋王后，王后似乎忽然裹在一團羊毛裡。愛麗絲揉揉眼睛，再看一次，完全無法理解到底發生了什麼事。她在一家店舖裡嗎？坐在櫃檯後面的……真的是……真的是一隻羊嗎？

愛麗絲再揉揉眼睛，仍搞不懂這是怎麼回事：她在一間陰暗的小店舖裡，手肘靠著櫃檯，櫃檯裡有隻老羊，牠正坐在扶手椅上打毛線，不時停下手邊的工作，透過一副大眼鏡打量她。

老羊停下手上的針織活，抬頭看著愛麗絲片刻，終於開口：「你想買什麼東西？」

愛麗絲很有禮貌地說：「嗯，我還不太確定。如果可以的話，我想先四處看一看。」

老羊說：「你喜歡的話，可以看看前面，看看兩邊，但你不可能四處看一看……除非你的後腦勺長了眼睛。」

愛麗絲的後腦勺確實沒長長眼睛，所以她只得轉身，看看一個個的貨架。

這間店鋪裡似乎充滿各種稀奇古怪的東西，但最奇怪的是，每次愛麗絲認真盯著某個貨架，想看清楚上面放了什麼東西，那個貨架就永遠空無一物，但旁邊的貨架卻塞滿東西。

她花了一分鐘左右的時間，盯著一個發亮的巨大東西，卻一直看不清楚。它有時看起來像洋娃娃，有時看起來像針線盒，總是出現她看的那個貨架的上一層。最後愛麗絲哀怨地說：「這裡的東西真會亂跑！這個東西最令人生氣……」這時她冒出一個念頭，補上一句：「但我有個主意，我要把它盯到最上面的貨架，它一定沒法穿透天花板！」

但就連這個計畫失敗了，那個「東西」無聲無息穿透了天花板，彷彿經常這麼做一樣。

老羊說：「你是小孩子還是陀螺啊？」牠拿起另一對棒針，「如果你再那樣轉下去，我的頭就快要昏了。」現在老羊用十四對棒針同時編織，愛麗絲驚訝萬分，忍不住一直盯著牠看。

困惑的愛麗絲心想：「牠怎麼能一次使用這麼多根棒針？牠越來越像一隻豪豬了！」

老羊問：「你會划船嗎？」牠遞給她兩根棒針。

愛麗絲開口：「會啊，會划一點點……」但不是在陸地上划……也不是用棒針划……」突然間，她手上的棒針變成了船槳，而且她發現自己與老羊坐在同一艘小船上，正沿著夾岸間的小河向前滑行。眼前沒有別的辦法，她只好努力划船。

老羊大喊：「平槳！」牠又拿起一對棒針。

這句話聽起來不像需要回答，所以愛麗絲沒說話，只是繼續划船。這條小河的水很古怪，因為船槳三不五時會被卡住，拔不出來。

愛麗絲心想：「可愛的小螃蟹（她把卡住聽成螃蟹了）！我想我應該會喜歡的。」

老羊再次大喊：「平槳！平槳！」牠拿起更多棒針，「船槳要卡住了。」

愛麗絲說：「我有聽到了呀，你講了很多次，而且還很大聲。請問螃蟹在哪裡？」

老羊氣得大吼：「你沒聽到我說『平槳』嗎？」牠拿起一堆棒針。

老羊說：「當然在水裡！」牠的雙手滿是棒針，所以把一些棒針插到頭髮裡，「我說的是平槳！」

愛麗絲終於很生氣地問：「為什麼你一直在說羽毛（她把平槳聽成羽毛了）？我又不是鳥！」

老羊說：「你是啊，你是小小呆頭鵝。」

愛麗絲有點惱怒，所以她和老羊好一會兒沒說話。小船緩緩流向前，有時漂進水草叢（船槳被水草緊緊卡在水裡，比先前更難拔出來），有時流過樹下，但總是與高高的河岸為伴，河岸彷彿皺眉盯著她們。

愛麗絲忽然欣喜若狂地大叫：「噢，拜託！那裡有些香香的燈心草！真的有，而且很漂亮！」

老羊說：「你不必為了那些燈心草來拜託我。」牠頭也不抬，繼續打毛線，「那些不是我種的，我也不會去摘。」

愛麗絲懇求：「不，我的意思是……拜託，我們可不可以停一下，摘些燈心草？你不介意把船停下來一會兒吧。」

老羊說：「我怎麼會有辦法把船停下來？只要你不要繼續划，船就會自己停了。」

於是小船隨著河水漂流，緩緩漂進擺蕩的燈心草叢。愛麗絲小心翼翼地捲高袖子，小小的手臂伸進水裡到手肘的深度，往下抓住燈心草，再把它們摘下

來。一時之間，愛麗絲完全忘了老羊與打毛線的事，她彎身探出船外，蓬亂的髮梢輕點水面，她睜著渴望的明亮眼睛，採下一把又一把美麗芳香的燈心草。

她自言自語：「但願不要翻船！噢，那株多麼可愛！只是我摘不到。」儘管隨著小船漂過，她摘了不少的燈心草，但總是有一株更漂亮的燈心草在她構不著的地方，這似乎確實有點氣人。（她心想：「簡直就像故意的！」）

最後，對於遙遠的固執燈心草，愛麗絲嘆氣說：「最漂亮的總是長得太遠！」她的雙頰紅潤，頭髮與雙手濕淋淋的。她爬回船上的位子，開始整理剛剛探下的寶貝。

愛麗絲採下燈心草的那一刻起，它們就開始凋萎，失去香氣與美麗，對她來說，這無關緊要。你知道的，即使是真正的燈心草，摘下來以後香氣也很短暫，何況這些是夢中的燈心草，堆在她腳邊的時候，就像雪一樣融化了。但愛麗絲並沒注意到這件事，她有許多稀奇古怪的事情要思索。

小船前進沒多久，一支船槳卡在水裡，再也不願意出來（後來愛麗絲這樣

解釋），結果槳柄打到愛麗絲的下巴，儘管可憐的她連續小聲尖叫著：「噢！噢！噢！」但依然被甩離位子，跌進那堆燈心草裡。

不過，她沒受傷，立刻又坐了起來。老羊一直打著毛線，彷彿什麼事都沒發生。愛麗絲坐回位子，很慶幸自己還在船上，這時老羊說：「這次船槳卡住得真棒啊！」

愛麗絲說：「是嗎？我沒看到螃蟹啊（她又把卡住聽成螃蟹了）。真希望沒讓牠跑了，真想帶隻小螃蟹回家！」她從船側謹慎地俯視幽暗的河水，

但老羊只是輕蔑一笑，繼續打毛線。

愛麗絲說：「這裡有很多螃蟹嗎？」

老羊說：「有螃蟹，還有各式各樣的東西。選擇很多，你只要拿定主意。好了，你究竟想買什麼？」

愛麗絲跟著說：「買！」她的語氣又驚又懼，因為船槳、小船、小河全都瞬間消失……她再度回到那間陰暗的小店鋪裡。

她怯生生地說：「我想買顆蛋，請問怎麼賣？」

老羊回答：「一顆蛋五又四分之一塊錢，兩顆蛋兩塊錢。」

愛麗絲驚訝地說：「兩顆比一顆便宜？」她拿出錢包。

老羊說：「但是如果你買兩顆，就必須把兩顆都吃掉。」

愛麗絲把錢放在櫃檯上，說道：「那我買一顆就好。」因為她心想……「或許不是每顆蛋都是好的。」

老羊收了錢，放進一個盒子裡，接著說：「我從來不把東西放在客人手上……那樣行不通，你得自己去拿。」說完，牠走到店舖後頭，把蛋立在一個貨架上。

愛麗絲心想：「奇怪，為什麼行不通？」因為通往店舖後面的通道非常昏暗，所以她一路摸索著桌椅前進。「我越是靠近，那顆蛋似乎就離得越遠。我看看，這是椅子嗎？哇！這張椅子有樹枝。天啊！這裡居然長出了樹，真是太奇怪了！而且這裡竟然還有一條小溪！哎呀，這是我見過最奇特的店舖！」

於是，愛麗絲繼續前進，越走越覺得驚奇……她經過的每樣東西都瞬間變成樹木，她想那顆蛋也不例外。

想一想

每次只要愛麗絲盯著店裡的東西看，商品就會消失，你覺得應該要怎麼做才能順利買到店舖裡的東西？

第六章　蛋頭先生

然而，那顆蛋越來越大，越來越像人的模樣。當愛麗絲走到離那顆蛋只有幾公尺的地方，她看到它有眼睛、鼻子、嘴巴。她再走近一點，看清楚那正是蛋頭先生。她自言自語：「不可能是別人！我很確定那就是他，他的臉上就像寫滿了名字一樣！」

那張臉龐龐大得可以輕輕鬆鬆寫上蛋頭先生的名字一百遍。蛋頭先生像土耳其人一樣盤腿坐在高牆上，那道牆很窄，愛麗絲很好奇他如何保持平衡的。蛋頭先生的眼睛一直盯著相反的方向，完全不理會愛麗絲，她覺得蛋頭先生一定是填充娃娃！

愛麗絲大聲說：「他完完全全像顆蛋！」她覺得蛋頭先生隨時都可能掉下

來，所以伸出雙手準備接住他。

蛋頭先生沉默許久才開口：「氣死我了，竟然被稱為蛋，真是氣死我了。」他說話時，完全不看愛麗絲一眼。

愛麗絲溫和地解釋：「先生，我是說你看起來像顆蛋了。」她補了一句：「有些蛋很漂亮。」她希望這能把剛才的話轉成讚美。

蛋頭先生依舊看也不看愛麗絲一眼，他說：「有些人的智慧，就跟嬰兒差不多。」

愛麗絲不知道該怎麼回應，她覺得這一切根本不像對話，因為蛋頭先生始終都沒對著她說話，事實上，他剛剛顯然是對著一棵樹講話。所以，愛麗絲站著那裡，柔聲背誦那首童謠給自己聽：

蛋頭先生坐牆上，

一不小心倒栽蔥，

國王所有的兵馬

沒法救起蛋頭先生。

愛麗絲大聲加上一句：「最後一行太長了，無法搭配這首詩。」她忘了蛋頭先生會聽到。

蛋頭先生說：「別站著那樣自言自語。」他第一次正眼看著愛麗絲，「報上你的姓名與目的。」

「我的名字是愛麗絲，但是……」

蛋頭先生不耐地打斷她：「眞是個蠢名字！這個名字代表什麼意義？」

愛麗絲懷疑地問：「名字一定要有意義嗎？」

蛋頭先生笑了一聲：「當然！我的名字表示了我的模樣，而且是很俊俏的模樣。你那種名字，幾乎可以用來表示任何模樣。」

愛麗絲不願跟他爭辯，她說：「爲什麼你一個人坐在這裡？」

蛋頭先生大聲說：「哼，因為沒人跟我在一起啊！你以為我不知道這個問題的答案嗎？下一題。」

愛麗絲接著說：「你不覺得待在地上比較安全嗎？」她沒想過編什麼謎語，只是好心為這個奇怪的生物擔心，「這道牆很窄！」

蛋頭先生咆哮著說：「你問的謎語太簡單了！我當然不覺得待在地上比較安全！哼，如果我真的摔下去……這種事根本不可能……但如果我摔下去……」他嚇起嘴巴，一臉嚴肅莊重，愛麗絲差點笑出來。他繼續說：「如果我摔下去，國王答應我……啊，你儘管臉色發白吧，隨便你！你覺得我不會那麼說吧？國王已經答應我，親口答應我……要……要……」

愛麗絲相當不智地插嘴：「派出他所有的兵馬。」

蛋頭先生忽然憤怒大喊：「我要說這太過分了！你一定躲在門外偷聽，躲在樹後偷聽，躲在煙囪裡偷聽！否則你不可能知道這件事！」

愛麗絲很溫和地說：「我真的沒偷聽！我在書上讀到的。」

蛋頭先生稍微冷靜地說：「好吧！他們確實可能把這種事寫在書裡，也就是所謂的『英國歷史』。現在，你仔細看看我！我可是跟國王說過話的人，我眞的是，或許你以後再也見不到這樣的人了！爲了表示我並不驕傲，你可以握握我的手！」他咧著嘴笑，嘴角幾乎咧到兩邊耳根，他彎著身子（差點

摔下牆了），伸出一隻手。愛麗絲握住他的手，有點焦慮地看著他，她心想：

「如果他笑得更開，兩個嘴角可能咧到腦後連在一起，到時不知道他的頭會怎麼樣！恐怕會掉下來！」

蛋頭先生繼續說：「對，國王所有的兵馬會立刻把我救起來，他們一定會的！不過我們聊得有點太快了，回到倒數第二個話題吧。」

愛麗絲彬彬有禮地說：「恐怕我記不起來是哪個話題了。」

蛋頭先生說：「那就重新開始吧，這次換我選話題了⋯⋯」（愛麗絲心想：「他講得好像玩遊戲一樣。」）「我問你，你剛剛說你幾歲了？」

愛麗絲很快地算了一下，接著回答：「七歲又六個月。」

蛋頭先生得意洋洋地大喊：「錯！你剛剛根本沒說過這樣的話！」

愛麗絲解釋：「我以為你的意思是問：『現在你幾歲了？』」

蛋頭先生說：「如果我是那個意思，我就會那樣問。」

愛麗絲不想再跟他爭辯，所以不說話。

蛋頭先生若有所思地複述一遍：「七歲又六個月！很棘手的年紀。如果你

先前徵詢我的意見，我會說：『停在七歲』，但現在為時已晚。」

愛麗絲憤怒地說：「我從來不為長大的事徵詢別人的意見！」

蛋頭先生說：「因為你太驕傲了？」

這句話讓愛麗絲更惱怒，她說：「我是指一個人沒辦法不長大。」

蛋頭先生說：「一個人可能沒辦法，但兩個人就有辦法了。有了適當的協

助，你或許就可以停在七歲。」

愛麗絲忽然說：「你的腰帶真漂亮！」（她覺得年齡的話題已經聊得夠多

了，如果他們真的要輪流選話題，現在該輪到她了。）她繼而一想，又趕緊更

正：「總之你的領巾很漂亮……不對，我是指腰帶……」她驚慌地補了一句：

「對不起！」因為蛋頭先生看起來徹底被惹惱了，她真希望自己剛剛沒選這個

話題，她心想：「真希望我分得出來哪裡是脖子、哪裡是腰！」

儘管蛋頭先生沉默了一兩分鐘，但他顯然氣得要命。等他再度開口時，變

成低聲咆哮。

他終於說話：「竟然連領巾與腰帶都分不清楚，真的是讓人……非常……

非常生氣！」

愛麗絲說：「我知道自己很無知。」她的語氣非常謙卑，蛋頭先生的氣消了一點。

「孩子，這是一條領巾。就像你所說的，這條領巾很漂亮，它是白棋國王與白棋王后送給我的禮物。你看！」

「真的嗎？」愛麗絲很高興地發現自己終究挑了好話題。

蛋頭先生翹著二郎腿，雙手抱著膝蓋，若有所思地繼續說：「他們送我這條領巾，當成非生日禮物。」

愛麗絲困惑地說：「不好意思，你說什麼？」

蛋頭先生說：「你又沒得罪我。」

「我的意思是，什麼是『非生日禮物』？」

「當然就是非生日的時候送的禮物。」

愛麗絲想了一下，最後說：「我最喜歡生日禮物了。」

蛋頭先生大聲說：「你根本不知道自己在說什麼！一年有幾天？」

愛麗絲說：「三百六十五天。」

「你一年有幾個生日？」

「一個。」

「三百六十五減掉一是多少？」

「當然是三百六十四。」

蛋頭先生一臉懷疑地說：「我要看你在紙上計算。」

愛麗絲忍不住笑出來，她拿出筆記本，寫出算式給他看：

$$\begin{array}{r} 365 \\ -1 \\ \hline 364 \end{array}$$

蛋頭先生接過筆記本，仔細地看，接著說：「算得似乎沒錯……」

愛麗絲插嘴：「你把筆記本拿反了！」

愛麗絲幫他把筆記本轉過來，蛋頭先生開心地說：「果真拿反了！難怪覺得看起來有點奇怪，就像我剛剛說的，算得似乎沒錯……雖然我剛剛沒時間徹底仔細檢查……這表示一年有三百六十四天可能收到非生日禮物……」

愛麗絲說：「的確。」

「一年只有一天能收到生日禮物，這就是你的榮耀。」

愛麗絲說：「我不懂你說的『榮耀』是什麼意思。」

蛋頭先生鄙夷地笑了，「你當然不懂啦，除非我告訴你。我的意思是，『你被無懈可擊的論點駁倒了！』」

愛麗絲抗議：「但『光榮』的意思又不是『無懈可擊的論點』。」

蛋頭先生以非常輕蔑的口氣說：「我用一個字詞的時候，我要它是什麼意思，它就是什麼意思，不多不少。」

愛麗絲說：「可是問題是，你是不是可以讓字詞包含那麼多的意思。」

蛋頭先生說：「問題是，誰是主人誰就可以，就這麼簡單。」

愛麗絲非常困惑，說不出話來。過了一會兒，蛋頭先生再度開口：「有些字詞的脾氣不太好……尤其是動詞，它們最驕傲……你可以對形容詞為所欲為，但對動詞可不行……不過，我可以管住它們！難以理解！我說了算！」

愛麗絲說：「請告訴我，那是什麼意思？」

蛋頭先生看起來非常高興，他說：「現在你說話像個懂事的孩子了。『難以理解』的意思就是，這個話題談得夠多了，你不妨說說看接下來打算做什麼，我想你也不打算一輩子都待在這裡吧。」

愛麗絲若有所思地說：「一個字詞要包含這麼多意思，真不容易。」

蛋頭先生說：「每當我讓一個字詞做那麼多工作的時候，總會多付一點錢給它們。」

愛麗絲說：「噢！」她一頭霧水，該不出話來。

蛋頭先生繼續說：「啊，你真該看看它們星期六晚上圍在我身邊的樣子，」他嚴肅地搖搖頭，「它們來領薪水，你懂的。」

（愛麗絲不敢問蛋頭先生用什麼付薪水，所以我也沒辦法告訴你。）

愛麗絲說：「先生，你似乎很擅長解釋字詞的意思，你願意為我解釋《查博蕪基龍》這首詩的意思嗎？」

蛋頭先生說：「唸來聽聽看。所有已經寫出來的詩我都能解釋，還沒寫出來的詩我也大多能解釋。」

聽起來很有希望，所以愛麗絲開始背誦第一段：

炙餐之刻，活滑類獾，
在圍緣螺轉錐鑽；
虛悲的布洛鳥，
迷家碧豕哨咆。

蛋頭先生打斷她：「先解釋這段就好，這段有很多難字。『炙餐之刻』指的是下午四點鐘，也就是開始燒烤食物當晚餐的時候。」

愛麗絲說：「解釋得很好。那『活滑』是什麼意思？」

「『活滑』指的是『柔軟又滑溜』，柔軟和『活躍』是相同的意思。你看，這個字就是混合詞，兩個意義合併成一個字。」

愛麗絲若有所思地說：「現在我懂了。那『類獾』是什麼呢？」

「嗯，『類獾』就是類似獾類的動物，有點像蜥蜴，又有點像螺絲錐。」

「牠們的長相一定很怪。」

蛋頭先生說：「確實是很怪，牠們在日晷儀下面做窩，以起司為食。」

「那『螺轉』與『錐鑽』是什麼意思呢？」

「『螺轉』是像陀螺儀那樣旋轉，『錐鑽』是像螺絲錐一樣打洞。」

愛麗絲說：「我猜『圍緣』就是圍繞著日晷儀的草地囉？」她很驚訝自己竟然那麼聰明。

「當然。這片草地被稱做『圍緣』就是因爲它延伸到前面很遠的地方，也延伸到後面很遠的地方⋯⋯」

愛麗絲補上一句：「還延伸到左右兩邊很遠的地方。」

「就是這樣。『虛悲』就是虛弱又可悲（你又學了一個混合詞），而『布洛鳥』是一種瘦弱難看的鳥，全身羽毛豎起來，就像一支活拖把。」

愛麗絲說：「那『迷家碧豕』呢？抱歉，給你添了很多麻煩。」

「嗯，『碧豕』是一種綠色的豬，但我不是很確定『迷家』的意思，我想那是『離家』的意思，表示牠們迷路回不了家。」

「那『哨咆』是什麼意思呢？」

「嗯，『哨咆』介於咆哮和吹口哨之間，還加上打噴嚏的聲音。你在那邊的森林裡或許會聽到這種聲音，你聽了會覺得很愉快。誰唸這麼難的東西給你聽的？」

愛麗絲說：「我在一本書裡讀到的，但我也聽過簡單多了的詩，我想應該

是崔德迪唸的。」

蛋頭先生說：「講到詩啊，你要知道，」他伸出一隻大手，「有必要的話，我可以背得跟其他人一樣好……」

愛麗絲趕緊說：「喔，沒必要的！」她希望阻止蛋頭先生唸詩。

「我要唸的這首詩，」蛋頭先生繼續往下說，沒理會愛麗絲的話，「完全是為了逗你開心而寫的。」

愛麗絲覺得既然如此，她真的必須聽一聽。她坐了下來，很憂愁地說了一聲「謝謝」。

冬季曠野白皚皚，
我唱此曲你開懷。

蛋頭先生補上一句解釋：「不過我不用唱的。」

愛麗絲說：「我看得出來你不用唱的。」

蛋頭先生很嚴厲地說：「如果你用看的就知道我到底有沒有唱，那麼你的眼力比大部分的人來得好。」

愛麗絲不說話。

我將盡訴心中事。

春日森林轉青翠，

愛麗絲說：「很感謝您。」

炎夏漫漫暑日長，

或許你將懂此曲……

金秋枝頭樹葉黃，

提筆蘸墨寫此曲。

蛋頭先生說：「你不要這樣子一直發表評論，你說的話沒什麼意義，而且還會打亂我。」

愛麗絲說：「如果那麼久之後我還記得的話，我會寫下來的。」

我捎信息給魚兒，

表明我的心願事。

海洋小魚得知後，

回覆訊息來給我。

小小魚兒回答我：

「我們真的辦不到⋯⋯」

愛麗絲說：「抱歉，我不太懂。」

蛋頭先生說：「後面比較好懂了。」

我又再度傳訊息，

「你們最好聽我話。」

小魚咧嘴笑著回：

「你的脾氣真是壞！」

我對牠們一再說，

牠們還是不肯聽。

我拿新的大水壺，

適合執行此任務。

我心狂擂怦怦跳，

唧筒抽水裝滿壺。

有人過來告訴我，

「小小魚兒已入睡。」

我很清楚告訴他，

「那你得叫醒牠們。」

我說得響亮清楚：

我在他耳邊大叫。

蛋頭先生唸到這一節的時候提高嗓音，幾乎就像尖叫。愛麗絲嚇得發抖，

她心想：「我絕對不願意當這個傳遞訊息的人！」

但他固執又驕傲：

說我不需對他吼！

但他驕傲又固執：

喚醒牠們有條件……

我從架上取螺錐，

親自喚醒小魚兒。

我發現牠們鎖門，拉推踢撞一起來。

我發現牠們關門，伸手扭了門把，卻⋯⋯

接著是一陣長長的沉默。

愛麗絲怯生生地問：「唸完了？」

蛋頭先生說：「唸完了，再見。」

愛麗絲心想，這真是突然，但他強烈暗示她該走了，再留下來實在太失禮了。

所以她站起來，伸出手，盡可能以最開朗的語氣道別：「下次見！」

蛋頭先生不滿地回答：「如果以後我們真的再見面，我應該不認得你，」他伸出一根手指與愛麗絲握手，「你的長相跟其他人一模一樣。」

愛麗絲若有所思地說：「我們通常是靠臉來認人。」

蛋頭先生說：「這就是我想抱怨的地方，你的臉跟所有人的臉都一樣：有兩個眼睛（他用大拇指在空中比出眼睛的位置），中間是鼻子，下面是嘴巴，總是一樣。比如說，如果你的兩個眼睛都長在鼻子的同一邊，或是嘴巴長在頭頂上……那可能比較好認。」

愛麗絲抗議：「那樣不好看。」

然而蛋頭先生閉上眼睛說：「等你試過再說吧。」

愛麗絲等了片刻，看看他是否還要再說什麼，但他一直沒張開眼睛，也沒理睬她。她再說了一次：「再見！」他還是沒回應，所以愛麗絲默默離開了。

但她一邊走，一邊忍不住自言自語：「在所有讓人不滿意的傢伙裡面（她又大聲說了一遍，因為能說出這麼長的句子是莫大的安慰），在我認識的、所有讓人不滿意的傢伙裡面……」但她的話沒說完，因為此時傳來重物落地的碎裂聲，震動整座森林。

想一想

如果有了蛋頭先生所說的「適當的協助」能夠不長大，你會想要停在自己幾歲的時候？為什麼？

第七章 獅子與獨角獸

緊接著，許多士兵狂奔穿越森林，起初是三三兩兩，接著是十位、二十位一起來……最後是一大群，整座森林似乎擠滿了人。愛麗絲怕被撞倒，於是躲到樹後看著他們跑過去。

愛麗絲這輩子還沒看過腳步這麼不穩的士兵：他們老是被東西絆倒，而且每次有一個人跌倒，總會有好幾個人跟著跌在他身上，因此不久後，森林裡到處都是跌成一小堆的士兵。

接著騎兵也來了。馬有四條腿，走得比步兵穩，但就連牠們也不時摔倒，而且每當馬一絆倒，馬背上的騎士就會立刻跌下來，似乎成了慣例。情況越來越混亂，愛麗絲趕緊跑出森林，來到一片空地，非常開心。她看到白棋國王坐

在地上，忙著寫筆記本。

白棋國王一見到愛麗絲，就開心大喊：「我把他們都派出去了！親愛的，你穿越森林的時候，有沒有遇到士兵啊？」

愛麗絲說：「有啊，我想應該有好幾千人吧。」

白棋國王看著筆記本說：「正確數字是四千兩百零七人。你知道，我不能把所有的馬都派出去，因為下棋的時候需要兩匹。我也沒派出兩名信差，他們都進城了。請你看看路上，有沒有看到哪個信差回來了？」

愛麗絲說：「我看到路上『沒人』。」

白棋國王焦躁地說：「真希望我有跟你一樣好的眼力，竟然能看到『沒人』！而且隔得這麼遠都還能看得到！唉，在這種光線之下，我最多只能看到『真人』！」

愛麗絲根本沒在聽國王說話，她的一隻手遮在眼睛上方，專心看著路上。

終於，她高聲喊著：「現在我看到她有人來了！但他走得很慢，姿勢也很奇

怪！」（因為那名信差不斷蹦蹦跳跳，又像鰻魚一樣扭動，兩隻大手在身側張開，就像兩把扇子。）

白棋國王說：「一點也不奇怪。他是盎格魯薩克遜信差，這就是盎格魯薩克遜姿勢，他只有開心的時候才會擺出那種姿勢，他的名字是海爾。」（國王這麼發音是為了與「梅爾」押韻。）

愛麗絲忍不住玩起字母接龍遊戲：「我喜愛名字 H 開頭的人，因為他叫做『歡喜』（Happy）。我討厭名字 H 開頭的人，因為他叫做『駭人』（Hideous）。我給他吃『火腿三明治』（ham-sandwiches）與很乾的『草』（hay）。他的名字是海爾，他住在……」

愛麗絲仍遲疑不決，還沒想出「H」開頭的小鎮名稱，白棋國王就接下去：「他住在『山丘』（hill）。」國王根本不知道自己無意中加入了遊戲，「另一個信差叫做海特。你知道的，我必須有兩位信差，一個來，一個去。」

愛麗絲說：「不好意思，你說什麼？」

白棋國王說：「乞求是不高尚的事。」

愛麗絲說：「我只是說我聽不懂而已，為什麼要一個來、一個去？」

白棋國王不耐地重複：「我不是跟你說過了嗎？我一定要有兩位信差，一個收信回來，一個送信過去。」

此時那位信差到了，他上氣不接下去，連話都說不出來，只能搖搖手，朝著可憐的白棋國王露出嚇人的表情。

白棋國王說：「這位年輕小姐喜歡你的名字中有個 H。」他介紹愛麗絲給信差認識，希望轉移信差對他的注意力。但是沒用……信差的盎格魯薩克遜姿勢越來越誇張，大眼睛拚命轉個不停。

白棋國王說：「你嚇壞我了！我快暈倒了……快給我一個火腿三明治！」

信差聽了就打開掛在脖子上的袋子，拿出一個火腿三明治給白棋國王，國王狼吞虎嚥地吃了下去，愛麗絲在旁邊興味盎然地看著。

白棋國王說：「再來一個！」

信差往袋子裡瞥了一眼：「沒了，只剩下乾草。」

白棋國王低聲喃喃：「那就給我乾草吧。」

愛麗絲很高興看到白棋國王吃了乾草後，精神好多了。白棋國王一邊津津有味地嚼著乾草，一邊告訴愛麗絲：「快昏倒的時候，沒有什麼像吃點乾草一樣。」

愛麗絲提議：「我覺得對你潑冷水會更好吧，或是聞點嗅鹽。」

白棋國王回答：「我並不是說沒有什麼比吃點乾草更好，我只是

說沒有什麼像吃點乾草這樣。」愛麗絲不敢反駁。

白棋國王再度伸手向信差要點乾草，繼續說：「你在路上遇到誰了嗎？」

信差說：「沒人。」

白棋國王說：「沒錯！這位年輕小姐也看到『沒人』，所以當然『沒人』走得比你慢？」

信差惱怒地說：「我盡力了，我敢說沒人走得比我快！」

白棋國王說：「他不可能走得比你快，否則他會比你先抵達。不過，既然你喘過氣來了，告訴我們城裡發生了什麼事吧。」

信差說：「我要小聲說。」他的手在嘴邊做成喇叭狀，彎腰湊近白棋國王的耳朵。愛麗絲覺得很惋惜，因為她也想聽聽消息。不過信差並未小聲說話，而是用最響亮的聲音吼著：「牠們又打起來了！」

可憐的白棋國王嚇得跳起來，渾身發抖，他大聲說：「這叫小聲嗎？如果你再這樣做，我就在你全身塗奶油！你的大嗓門簡直像地震一樣，讓我腦袋轟

隆作響！」

愛麗絲心想：「那一定是場很小的地震吧！」她鼓起勇氣問：「誰又打起來了？」

白棋國王說：「啊，當然是獅子與獨角獸。」

「為了爭王冠嗎？」

白棋國王說：「對，沒錯。最好笑的是，那頂王冠一直是我的！我們跑過去看看吧。」

他們邁步往前跑，愛麗絲一邊跑，一邊背誦那首古老的童謠：

獅子與獨角獸打架爭王冠；
獅子把獨角獸打得滿城亂跑，
有人給白麵包也有人給黑麵包。
有人給水果蛋糕，打鼓趕牠們出城。

愛麗絲跑得氣喘吁吁，努力擠出問句：「是不是……贏的那方……就會得到王冠？」

白棋國王說：「天啊，不可能！真是荒唐的想法！」

愛麗絲又跑了一會兒後，她喘著氣說：「能不能請你……行行好……停下一分鐘……讓我喘口氣……」

白棋國王說：「我是很好，只是我不夠強壯。你看，一分鐘過得快得嚇人，根本攔不住，倒不如試著擋住邦德斯納獸算了！」

愛麗絲喘得沒辦法說話，於是他們默默奔跑，直到看見一大群人，獅子與獨角獸在人群中間打架，周圍滿天塵土飛揚。起初愛麗絲根本分不出誰是誰，但她很快就靠著犄角認出了獨角獸。

他們走到另一位信差海特身邊，海特站著觀戰，一手拿著一杯茶，一手拿著奶油麵包。

海爾低聲告訴愛麗絲：「他剛出獄，當初他被關進去的時候，茶都沒喝完

呢。監獄裡的人只給他吃牡蠣殼，所以你看，他又餓又渴。」

海爾親暱地摟住海特的脖子說：

「小兄弟，你好嗎？」

海特回頭看了一眼，點點頭，繼續吃奶油麵包。

海爾說：「小兄弟，你在牢裡開不開心？」

海特再度看了一下，這次一、兩滴眼淚流下他的臉頰，但他還是不說話。

海爾不耐地大吼：「說話啊，你不會說話嗎！」但海特只是繼續嚼著麵包，又喝了幾口茶。

白棋國王大聲說：「快說話！牠們打得怎麼樣了？」

海特費了很大的勁，吞下一大塊奶油麵包，他用哽住的聲音說：「牠們打得很好，兩方各被擊倒八十七次左右。」

愛麗絲鼓起勇氣說：「那麼，我想很快就有人拿白麵包與黑麵包來了？」

海特說：「麵包已經等著牠們了，現在我吃的這塊就是。」

這時打鬥暫停，獅子與獨角獸坐下來喘氣，白棋國王高喊：「休息十分鐘吃點心！」海爾與海特立刻開始忙碌，端著一盤盤的白麵包與黑麵包到處分送。愛麗絲拿了一塊品嚐，但麵包很乾。

白棋國王對海特說：「我想牠們今天不會再打了，傳令開始打鼓吧。」海特像隻炸蜢一樣蹦蹦跳跳地走了。

愛麗絲默默站了一兩分鐘，看著海特離開。忽然間，她露出喜色，急切指著某個方向大喊：「快看，快看！白棋王后跑過田野了！她從那邊的森林裡飛奔出來的……那些王后跑得真快啊！」

白棋國王說：「一定有敵人在追她。」他根本沒轉頭看一眼，「森林裡充滿敵人。」

愛麗絲問：「你不跑去幫她嗎？」白棋國王非常平靜，愛麗絲很詫異。

白棋國王說：「沒用的，沒用的！她跑起來快得嚇人，倒不如試著抓住邦德斯納獸算了！不過如果你喜歡的話，我會把她的事記在筆記本裡……」他打開筆記本，輕聲自言自語：「她是可愛的好人，對吧？『人』要怎麼寫？」

此時獨角獸漫步走到他們旁邊，雙手插在口袋裡。牠經過白棋國王的身邊時，瞥了他一眼，說道：「這次我獲勝了吧？」

白棋國王相當緊張地回答：「一點點……一點點。但你不該用角頂牠，你知道的。」

獨角獸不在乎地說：「那又沒傷到牠。」牠準備離開時，目光剛好落在愛麗絲身上，牠立刻轉身，露出極度厭惡的表情，盯著她看了好一會兒。

獨角獸最後說：「這……是……什麼東西？」

海爾熱切地回答：「這是個小孩！」他走到愛麗絲前面，張開雙手，用盎

格魯薩克遜姿勢介紹她，「我們今天才發現的，她跟眞人一樣大，而且還非常

天然！」

獨角獸說：「我一直以爲小孩是傳說中的怪物！她是活的嗎？」

海爾嚴肅地說：「她還會說話！」

獨角獸出神看著愛麗絲：「小孩，說話。」

愛麗絲忍不住彎起嘴角，微笑著說：「你知道嗎？我也一直以爲獨角獸是

傳說中的怪物！我從來沒看過活生生的獨角獸！」

獨角獸說：「好吧，既然我們已經見過面了，如果你相信我存在，我就相

信你存在，就這樣說定了？」

愛麗絲說：「好，就照你的意思。」

獨角獸的目光從愛麗絲身上移向白棋國王：「老頭，快點拿出水果蛋糕！

我才不吃你們的黑麵包！」

白棋國王低聲說：「沒問題，沒問題！」他低聲向海爾示意：「打開袋子！快一點！不是那個……那裡面都是乾草！」

海爾從袋子裡拿出一個大蛋糕，交給愛麗絲拿著，接著拿出盤子與切片刀。愛麗絲猜不透那個袋子怎麼拿得出那麼多東西，她想這或許就像變魔術。

這時獅子也加入他們，牠看起來筋疲力盡，昏昏欲睡，眼睛快閉起來了。牠懶洋洋地眨著眼睛，看著愛麗絲說：

「這是什麼東西！」牠的聲音低沉迴盪，聽起來像巨鐘的鐘聲。

獨角獸熱切地高聲說：「啊！這是什麼東西？你絕對猜不到！我剛剛也沒猜出來。」

獅子疲倦地看著愛麗絲說：「你是動物？植物？還是礦物？」他每說兩個字就打個呵欠。

愛麗絲還來不及回答，獨角獸就大聲說：「這是傳說中的怪物！」

獅子說：「怪物，你過來分水果蛋糕吧。」牠趴下來，下巴擱在前爪上，（對著白棋國王與獨角獸說：）「你們兩個坐下吧。你們知道的，分蛋糕要公平！」

白棋國王不得不坐在兩隻巨獸中間，他看起來顯得很不自在，但沒有其他位子能坐。

獨角獸狡猾地看著白棋國王的王冠，說道：「我們再打一架搶王冠好了，現在就打！」

可憐的國王全身抖得厲害，腦袋都快抖掉了。

獅子說：「我輕輕鬆鬆就能贏你。」

獨角獸說：「那可不一定。」

獅子挺起上半身，憤怒地回答：「哼，那我就把你打得滿城跑，你這個膽小鬼！」

獨角獸說：「那可不一定。」

獅子說：「我輕輕鬆鬆就能贏你。」

此時白棋國王為了阻止牠們繼續爭執，於是插嘴：「滿城跑嗎？那可是很長的一條路呢，你們經過了舊橋或市場呢？舊橋賞景最美了。」他緊張得要命，聲音顫抖。

獅子再度趴下來，低吼著說：「我確定自己不知道，滿天都是塵土，看不見任何東西。那個怪物切個蛋糕怎麼切這麼久！」

愛麗絲坐在小溪邊，大盤子放在膝蓋上，拿著刀子努力地切蛋糕。她回答獅子：「氣死人了！（她已經很習慣被稱為『怪物』了）我剛剛切了好幾片，但每片總是又合起來！」

獨角獸說：「你不知道怎麼切鏡中的蛋糕，要先分給大家，然後再切。」

這聽起來是胡說八道，但愛麗絲聽話地站起來，拿著盤子繞著大家走一圈，蛋糕就自動分成三片了。等到愛麗絲拿著空盤子回到原位，獅子說：「現在快切吧。」

坐著的愛麗絲拿著刀子，非常困惑，不知道怎麼開始切，這時獨角獸大聲說：「喂！這不公平！這個怪物給獅子的蛋糕大小，是我的兩倍！」

獅子說：「可是不管怎麼說，她沒留任何蛋糕給自己。怪物，你喜歡水果蛋糕嗎？」

但愛麗絲還來不及回答，鼓聲就響了。

她聽不出鼓聲從哪裡傳來，空氣中充滿鼓聲，那聲音在她腦中不斷迴盪，她覺得快聾了。

她嚇得站起來，驚恐地跳過小溪。

匆忙之間，她看見獅子與獨角獸站了起來，因為饗宴被打斷而一臉憤怒。

接著她跪下來，雙手摀住耳朵，想擋住那可怕的噪音，卻徒勞無功。

愛麗絲心想：

「如果那鼓聲還不能把牠們趕出城的話，也沒別的辦法了！」

獨角獸對愛麗絲說：「如果你相信我存在，我就相信你存在。」那如果愛麗絲不相信獨角獸存在，愛麗絲就不存在了嗎？

第八章 「這是我的發明」

過了一會兒，鼓聲似乎漸漸停止，最後一片死寂。愛麗絲有點不安地抬起頭，沒看見任何人。她第一個想法是自己一定在做夢，夢到了獅子、獨角獸、兩位古怪的盎格魯薩克遜信差，但那個裝水果蛋糕的大盤子還擱在她的腳邊。

她自言自語：「所以我不是在做夢，除非……除非我們都在同一個夢裡，但我希望這是我的夢，不是紅棋國王的夢！我不喜歡在別人的夢裡。」她以抱怨的語氣繼續說：「我真想叫醒他，看看會發生什麼事！」

此時她的思緒被打斷，有人大喊：「喝呀！喝呀！停！」穿著深紅色盔甲的一位騎士策馬奔馳，衝向愛麗絲，手中揮著一根大棍棒；就在他衝到她面前時，馬兒突然停住，他摔下馬背，大喊：「你是我的俘虜！」

愛麗絲嚇了一跳，但更為騎士擔心，有點不安地看著他重新騎上馬。騎士坐穩在馬鞍上之後，立刻又開始大喊：「你是我的……」這時卻被另一道聲音打斷：「喝呀！喝呀！停！」愛麗絲驚訝地環顧四周，尋找新來的敵人。

這次是一位白棋騎士，他勒馬停在愛麗絲旁邊，像紅棋騎士一樣摔下馬，接著又爬上去坐好。兩位騎士坐

在馬背上，盯著彼此，好一會兒都沒說話。愛麗絲看看這位，又看看那位，一頭霧水。

紅棋騎士終於開口：「你知道的，她是我的俘虜！」

白棋騎士回答：「對，但我來救她了！」

紅棋騎士說：「嗯，那我們勢必要為她打上一仗了！」他拿起頭盔戴上。

（頭盔掛在馬鞍上，形狀是馬頭。）

白棋騎士也戴上頭盔說：「你會遵守戰鬥規則吧？」

紅棋騎士說：「一向如此。」接著他們怒沖沖地開打了，愛麗絲躲到樹後，以免遭受池魚之殃。

愛麗絲一邊在藏身的地方膽怯地偷看這場戰鬥，一邊自言自語：「我真想知道戰鬥的規則，其中一條規則似乎是如果一位騎士打中另一位騎士，就要把對方打下馬，如果沒打中，就得自己滾下馬。另一條規則似乎是騎士得用雙臂抱住棍棒，彷彿是木偶戲《潘趣與茱迪》的主角。他們摔下馬的聲音真大聲！

就像整組火爐用具都掉進壁爐圍欄！那兩匹馬真安靜！任由那兩位騎士爬上爬下，彷彿牠們是桌子一樣！」

愛麗絲沒注意到，另一條規則似乎是騎士摔下馬時總是頭先著地，當兩人一起倒栽蔥跌下馬來，戰鬥就結束了。他們再度爬起來，握握手，接著紅棋騎士跨上馬，策馬疾馳離開。

白棋騎士氣喘吁吁走過來說：「這是光榮的勝利，對吧？」

愛麗絲不確定地說：「我不知道。我不想當俘虜，我想當王后。」

白棋騎士說：「你越過下一條小溪後，就變成王后了。我會護送你平安抵達森林盡頭⋯⋯然後我就得回頭，你懂的，我這一步只能走到那裡。」

愛麗絲說：「非常謝謝你，需要我幫你脫掉頭盔嗎？」白棋騎士顯然無法自行脫掉，但愛麗絲也費了一番力氣才幫他卸下頭盔。

白棋騎士說：「現在呼吸輕鬆多了！」他的雙手把蓬亂的頭髮往後撥，溫和的臉龐轉向愛麗絲，溫柔的大眼睛看著她。愛麗絲心想，她從沒見過長相如

此奇怪的士兵。

白棋騎士穿著似乎極不合身的錫製盔甲，肩上掛著一個模樣古怪的小木箱，箱子上下顛倒，箱蓋打開懸著。愛麗絲很好奇地看著小木箱。

白棋騎士友善地說：「我看見你在欣賞我的小箱子，這是我的發明，用來裝衣服與三明治。你看，我倒著揹，這樣雨水就進不去了。」

愛麗絲輕聲說：「但是東西會掉出來，你知道蓋子開著嗎？」

白棋騎士說：「我不知道。」他的臉上閃過一絲惱怒，「那麼裡面的東西一定全都掉光了！沒了裡頭的東西，這個箱子也沒用了。」說著他就解下箱子，準備丟到矮樹叢裡，但似乎又忽然想到一個點子，於是他小心翼翼地將箱子掛在樹上。他問愛麗絲：「你猜得到為什麼我要這麼做嗎？」

愛麗絲搖搖頭。

「我希望蜜蜂在裡面築巢，這樣我就能採蜂蜜了。」

愛麗絲說：「但是你的馬鞍上已經綁了一個蜂窩，或者像蜂窩的東西。」

白棋騎士不滿意地說：「對，那個蜂窩很棒，上好的蜂窩，但沒有任何一隻蜜蜂靠近過。另一樣東西是捕鼠器，我猜老鼠嚇跑了蜜蜂，或者蜜蜂嚇跑了老鼠，我不知道究竟是誰嚇跑誰。」

愛麗絲問：「我很好奇捕鼠器有什麼用，馬背上不太可能有老鼠吧。」

白棋騎士說：「或許不太可能，但萬一老鼠真的來了，我可不想讓牠們四

處亂跑。」

沉默片刻後，他繼續說：「你懂的，凡事最好有備無患，所以我的馬兒四隻腳上都套著刺環。」

愛麗絲很好奇地問：「但刺環的用途是什麼？」

白棋騎士回答：「用來防止被鯊魚咬，這也是我的發明。現在請扶我上馬，我陪你走到森林盡頭。這個盤子的用途是什麼？」

愛麗絲說：「原本是用來裝水果蛋糕。」

白棋騎士說：「我們最好帶著它，如果我們找到水果蛋糕，它就能派上用場了。請協助我把它放進這個袋子裡。」

雖然愛麗絲小心翼翼地撐開袋子，但他們還是花了很久的時間，才把盤子裝進去，因為白棋騎士非常笨手笨腳，頭兩三次嘗試時甚至自己跌進袋子裡。等他們終於把盤子裝進袋子裡，白棋騎士說：「你看，這個袋子裝得很滿了，裡面有很多燭臺。」他把袋子掛在馬鞍上，馬鞍上早就掛了幾串胡蘿蔔與火爐

用具，還有一大堆東西。

他們出發時，白棋騎士繼續說：「我想你的頭髮綁得很牢吧？」

愛麗絲微笑著說：「就跟平常一樣。」

白棋騎士焦急地說：「那樣不夠。這裡的風猛得跟猛虎一樣猛。」

愛麗絲問：「你有沒有什麼發明能讓頭髮不被風吹散？」

白棋騎士說：「沒有。但我有個方法可以讓頭髮不會往下掉。」

「我很想聽聽看。」

白棋騎士說：「首先你在頭上豎根棍子，再把頭髮往上繞在棍子上，就像果樹一樣。你知道的，頭髮會往下掉是因為它垂下來，但東西絕對不會往上掉落。這是我的發明，如果你願意的話，可以試試看。」

愛麗絲覺得這個方法聽起來很不舒服，她一邊靜靜往前走了幾分鐘，一邊苦苦思索這個方法，並不時停下來幫助這名可憐的白棋騎士，因為他真的不是出色的騎士。每次馬兒一停（牠三不五時就停下來），白棋騎士就會往前摔下

馬；每次馬兒再度往前走（牠通常都突然起步），白棋騎士就會往後栽下馬。

除此之外，他騎得還不錯，只是他習慣從側邊摔下馬，而且通常往愛麗絲那邊摔，愛麗絲很快就發現最好不要太靠近馬兒。

愛麗絲第五次扶著白棋騎士上馬時鼓起勇氣說：「恐怕您還要多練習。」

白棋騎士聽了這句話，他面露訝異，而且有些惱怒。他問：「為什麼你會這樣說？」他爬回馬鞍上，一手抓著愛麗絲的頭髮，以免從另外一邊摔下去。

「因為人們多加練習的話，就不會經常摔下來。」

白棋騎士非常嚴肅地說：「我練得很多，練得很多。」

愛麗絲說：「真的嗎？」除了這句話，她想不到更好的回應，但盡可能說得很真誠。他們又默默走了一小段路，白棋騎士閉著眼自言自語，愛麗絲看著他，擔心他再摔下來。白棋騎士忽然揮舞右臂，大聲說：「騎馬的偉大藝術在於保持……」他講到一半忽然中斷，因為他又以倒栽蔥的姿勢摔下馬，跌在愛麗絲面前。愛麗絲這次嚇壞了，她扶他起來並焦慮地問：「沒摔斷骨頭吧？」

白棋騎士說：「小事，不值得一提。」彷彿摔斷兩三根骨頭也不在意，「就像我剛剛說的，騎馬的偉大藝術在於保持平衡，你懂的，就像這樣……」

白棋騎士放開韁繩，張開雙臂，爲愛麗絲示範那句話的意思。這次他摔得仰躺在地，就摔在馬兒腳邊。

愛麗絲扶他站起來的時候，他不停重複說著：「練得很多！練得很多！」

這次愛麗絲終於失去耐心，大聲地說：「這太可笑了！你應該騎那種有輪子的木馬，眞的！」

白棋騎士很感興趣地問：「那種木馬跑起來平穩嗎？」他邊說邊緊抱著馬兒脖子，總算及時救了自己一次，沒再摔下馬。

愛麗絲說：「那比活生生的馬兒平穩多了。」儘管她很努力忍住笑意，卻還是小聲笑了出來。

白棋騎士若有所思地自言自語：「我要弄個一匹，一匹或兩匹吧，弄個幾匹好了。」

白棋騎士說完就沉默片刻，接著又說：「我很擅長發明東西。我猜你剛才扶我起來的時候，一定有注意到我沉思的表情吧？」

愛麗絲說：「你看起來確實有點嚴肅。」

「嗯，那時我正在發明越過柵欄門的新方法，你想聽嗎？」

愛麗絲禮貌地說：「非常想聽。」

白棋騎士說：「我跟你說我怎麼想到這個辦法的，你懂的，我告訴自己：『唯一的難題是腳，因為頭夠高了。』所以，我先把頭放在柵欄門上，這樣頭就夠高了，我再倒立，這樣腳也夠高了，你看，我就越過柵欄門了。」

愛麗絲若有所思地說：「對，我想這樣你就能越過柵欄門了，但你不覺得這個方法很困難嗎？」

白棋騎士嚴肅地說：「我還沒試過，所以無法確定，但恐怕會有點困難。」

他看起來很煩惱，所以愛麗絲趕緊換個話題，她用愉快的語氣說：「你的頭盔好特別！它也是你的發明嗎？」

白棋騎士自豪地低頭看著掛在馬鞍上的頭盔，說道：「對。但我發明過更好的頭盔，那個頭盔看起來像圓錐狀的糖，當我戴著那個頭盔，要是摔下馬，進頭盔總是先著地，所以摔下來的距離就變得很短了。但風險是有時整個人會掉進頭盔裡，有一次我就發生這樣的事，最糟的是我還來不及爬出來，另一位白棋騎士路過就撿起來戴上，以為那是他的頭盔。」

白棋騎士看起來很嚴肅，愛麗絲不敢笑，她用顫抖的聲音說：「你就在他頭頂上，一定弄傷他了吧。」

白棋騎士非常認真地說：「我當然得踢他，接著他才把頭盔脫掉，但是我花了好幾個鐘頭才爬出來。你知道的，我快得……跟閃電一樣！」

愛麗絲反駁：「但那種快不一樣。」

白棋騎士搖搖頭說：「我可以向你保證，那是我最快的動作了！」他邊說邊激動地舉起雙手，結果立刻從馬鞍上滾落，倒栽蔥跌進深溝裡。

愛麗絲跑到深溝旁找他，這次她吃了一驚，因為他已經好一會兒都騎得很

平穩。愛麗絲擔心他這次真的摔傷了。

不過，雖然愛麗絲只能看到他的鞋底，但聽他說話的語氣跟平常一樣，她鬆了一口氣。白棋騎士又說了一次：「那是我最快的動作了。但那個騎士太粗心大意了，竟然戴了別人的頭盔，還連人帶帽一起戴。」

愛麗絲問：「你頭下腳上的時候，怎麼能夠這麼平靜地講話？」她抓住白棋騎士的腳，把他拖出深溝，讓他坐在溝邊的土堆上。

聽了這個問題，白棋騎士一臉驚訝地說：「我的姿勢跟說話有什麼關係？

我的頭腦一樣在運作啊。事實上，我越是頭上腳下，就越能發明新東西。」

他沉默片刻後又說：「我發明的東西中，最絕妙的就是吃肉類主菜時發明的新布丁。」

愛麗絲說：「及時煮了當成下一道菜嗎？嗯，那無疑是真的很快！」

白棋騎士以若有所思的語氣緩緩說：「嗯，不是下一道菜，不是，當然不是下一道菜。」

「那一定是第二天吃囉，我想你不會一頓晚餐吃兩道布丁吧？」

白棋騎士同樣緩緩地說：「嗯，不是第二天，不是第二天。」他低下頭，聲音越來越低，繼續說：「事實上，我想那種布丁從來沒人做過！事實上，我想將來也不會有人做！但那仍是絕妙的布丁。」

愛麗絲問：「你發明的那種布丁是什麼做的？」愛麗絲想為白棋騎士打氣，因為他看起來心情非常低落。

白棋騎士咕噥著說：「先用吸墨紙……」

「恐怕不是很好吃……」

白棋騎士很急切打斷她：「單吃是不太好吃，但你絕對想不到，它跟其他東西混在一起，例如火藥與封蠟，味道就完全不同了。我必須在這裡向你告別了。」他們已經抵達森林的盡頭。

愛麗絲只是一臉困惑，仍想著那種布丁。

白棋騎士擔心地說：「你看起來一臉悲傷，我唱首歌安慰你吧。」

愛麗絲問：「很長嗎？」因為這天她已經聽過很多首詩。

白棋騎士說：「很長，但這首歌非常非常美麗。每個聽過我唱這首歌的人，不是掉眼淚，就是……」

愛麗絲問：「就是怎樣？」因為白棋騎士說到一半就忽然打住。

「就是沒掉眼淚。這首歌被稱為《黑線鱈的眼睛》。」

愛麗絲說：「噢，那就是歌名，對嗎？」她努力裝出很感興趣的樣子。

白棋騎士看起來有點惱怒，他說：「不對，你沒弄懂，這首歌被稱為《黑

線鱈的眼睛》，但真正的歌名其實是《很老的老頭》。」

愛麗絲改口：「所以我應該說『這首歌被稱為《黑線鱈的眼睛》囉？』」

「不，你不應該這麼說，那是兩碼子事！這首歌被稱為《方式與方法》，但那只是個說法而已，你懂的！」

此時愛麗絲一頭霧水，她說：「嗯，這首歌的歌名究竟是什麼呢？」

白棋騎士說：「我正要說呢，這首歌的歌名其實是《坐在柵欄門上》，曲調是我寫的。」

說到這裡，白棋騎士勒馬停下，任由韁繩落在馬兒的頸邊。接著，他一隻手慢慢打拍子，一抹淺笑讓他溫和傻氣的臉龐亮了起來，他彷彿沉醉在自己的曲子中，接著開始唱了起來。

在這趟穿越鏡子之旅裡，愛麗絲經歷了各種稀奇古怪的事情，但這個場景她永遠記得最清楚，多年後，她依舊能回想起這整個情景，一切歷歷如昨：白棋騎士溫柔的藍色眼眸與親切的微笑，夕陽照得他的髮絲閃著微光，映得他的

盔甲閃閃發亮，讓愛麗絲一時睜不開眼睛；馬兒靜靜地隨處走走，韁繩鬆鬆地掛在牠的頸邊，低頭在愛麗絲腳邊吃草，襯著後方森林的幽暗影子，她眼前的這一切彷彿一幅畫。

愛麗絲一隻手遮在眼睛上方，倚靠著樹，望著這一對奇異的騎士與馬兒，如夢似醒地聽著這首歌的哀傷曲調。

她自言自語：「但這曲子不是他編的啊，這首曲子是《一切獻給你，我一無所有》。」她站著專心聽歌，但沒有流淚。

我問老翁是何人？

坐在柵欄門上頭。

我看見一位老翁，

儘管沒什麼可說。

我願告訴你一切，

做何營生過日子？

他的話如水過篩，

網不住啊記不得。

他說捕蝶過生活，

日日尋蝶麥田裡。

蝴蝶加進羊肉派，

拿到大街上兜售。

販賣派餅給水手，

波浪滔天出海苦。

靠著此法來營生，

賺得小錢過日子。

但我滿腦子盤算，

要將鬍子來染綠，

再用一把大扇子，

不讓人見遮鬍子。

我沒專心聽他說，

沉默以對無回應，

一拳搥在他腦袋，

追問他怎麼過活！

老翁柔聲說從頭，

為了生活忙奔走，

找到山上的小溪，

放火燒乾小溪水，

好不容易來做成，

羅蘭牌的護髮油。

辛辛苦苦的代價，

只得銅板一塊半。

但我一心想法子，

靠著麵糊來果腹，

過了一日又一日，

養得身體胖嘟嘟。

我抓老翁左右搖，

搖得他臉色發青。

我問他靠何營生，

究竟怎麼過日子！

他說石楠叢裡找，
尋覓黑線鱈眼睛，
夜半無聲雕魚眼，
做成背心的鈕扣。
魚眼鈕扣價不高，
不需黃金或銀幣，
只要半塊錢銅幣，
即可買下九粒扣。

不時挖奶油餐包，
樹枝塗膠黏螃蟹。
不時尋覓草坡上，
撿拾雙輪馬車輪。

老翁朝我眨眨眼，
他靠此法賺大錢。
舉杯歡喜敬一杯，
祝君永遠保安康。

我聽他說完故事，
心中已然有盤算，
葡萄酒煮美奈橋，
就能避免橋生鏽。
誠心感謝他分享，
說出發財致富法，
實為感謝他祝福，
祝我永遠保安康。

每當不慎出錯誤，
手指塞進漿糊裡，
或是一時犯糊塗，
右腳塞進左鞋裡，
或是重物往下掉，
砸到我的腳趾上，
總令我淚流滿面，
因為想起此老翁……

面容溫和說話慢，
頭髮瑩白勝雪花，
模樣長得像烏鴉，
眼神灼亮似炭火，

他坐在柵欄門上。

多年前那個夏夜，

他的鼾聲如水牛，

彷彿嘴裡含麵團，

喃喃低語聽不清，

身軀來回搖不停，

憂傷心事盈滿懷，

白棋騎士唱完最後一句，抓起韁繩，調轉馬頭朝著剛剛走來的那條路。他說：「你只剩下幾公尺的路要走，走下山坡，越過小溪，你就變成王后了。」

愛麗絲一臉期待地轉頭看著白棋騎士指的方向，白棋騎士補充說：「你願不願意先在這裡待一會兒，目送我離開？不會很久的，只要等我走到那個轉彎的地方，你向我揮揮手帕就好了！這樣能鼓勵我。」

愛麗絲說：「當然願意。非常感謝你陪我走了這麼遠，也謝謝你唱歌給我聽，我很喜歡這首歌。」

白棋騎士懷疑地說：「希望如此。但你沒哭，我以為你會淚流滿面。」

他們握握手之後，白棋騎士騎馬緩緩進入森林。愛麗絲一邊站著目送白棋騎士離開，一邊自言自語：「我想目送他離開不會花太多時間。他又摔下馬了！還是頭先著地！但他又輕鬆地爬上馬……都是因為馬兒的身上掛了很多東西……」愛麗絲一邊自言自語，一邊看著馬兒慢悠悠地沿著路前進。白棋騎士不斷滾下馬，一下從左側摔下來，一下從右側摔下來，摔了第四次或第五次後，終於到了轉彎處。愛麗絲朝著他揮揮手帕，直到他的身影消失。

愛麗絲說：「我希望這樣鼓勵了他。」她轉身衝下山，「現在越過最後一條小溪，我就變成王后了！聽起來真是了不起！」她跑了幾步就到了溪邊，大喊著跳過小溪：「終於到了第八格！」

她撲倒在草地上歇息，草地柔軟得像苔蘚一樣，四處點綴著一小叢一小叢

的花兒。「噢，真開心來到這裡！」她忽然驚訝大喊：「我頭上是什麼東西啊？」她伸出雙手去摸，有個極沉重的東西緊緊套住她的頭。

愛麗絲自言自語：「但它是怎麼不知不覺跑到我頭上的？」她把頭上的東西拿下來放在大腿上，看看它到底是什麼玩意兒。

原來是一頂黃金王冠。

想一想

你覺得為什麼即使白棋騎士這樣摔了又摔，仍堅持護送愛麗絲走到下一格？

第九章　愛麗絲王后

愛麗絲說：「哇！太棒了！我從沒想過這麼快就當上王后了……」她用嚴厲的語氣說（她向來喜歡責罵自己）：「王后陛下，請容我說一句，你那樣懶洋洋地躺在草地上實在不像話！你知道的，當王后必須高貴莊重！」

所以她站起來四處走走，起初因為擔心王冠會掉下來，走得很僵硬。但她心想沒人會看到，就寬心多了，於是又坐了下來，說道：「如果我眞的成了王后，遲早會習慣的。」

這裡發生的每件事都很奇怪，所以當愛麗絲發現紅棋王后與白棋王后分別坐在她的左右兩側，她一點都不驚訝。她很想問問她們是怎麼來的，但擔心這樣很失禮。不過她心想，詢問棋局是否結束了，應該無傷大雅。她怯生生地看

著紅棋王后說：「請問一下，能不能請你……」

紅棋王后嚴厲地打斷她：「有人先跟你說話，你才可以說話！」

愛麗絲一向隨時準備跟人爭論一下：「但如果每個人都遵守這個規矩，一定要別人先跟你說話，你才能說話，而對方也一直在等你先開口，這樣大家永遠都不用說話了，這樣子一來……」

紅棋王后大喊：「荒謬！哼，你這孩子，難道不知道……」這時她忽然皺眉打住話頭，想了一會兒後，忽

然換了話題：「你剛才說『如果我真的成了王后』是什麼意思？你有什麼資格這樣稱呼自己？除非通過正式考試，否則你不能當王后，知道嗎？我們越快開始越好。」

可憐的愛麗絲哀怨地辯解：「我只是說『如果』！」

兩位王后互相看了對方一眼，紅棋王后微微顫抖地說：「她說她只是說『如果』……」

白棋王后扭著雙手，不滿地抱怨：「但她說的比那多得多！喔，比那多了許多！」

紅棋王后對愛麗絲說：「所以你知道，你真的說了很多。永遠要說實話……說話前先三思，說完後寫下來。」

「我很確定自己沒有意思要……」愛麗絲才開口，但紅棋王后不耐煩地打斷她。

「這就是我不滿的地方！你說話應該要有意思！你覺得沒有意思的小孩有

什麼用？就連笑話都應該有意思，我想一個小孩比一個笑話來得重要。你無法否認這一點，就算用上雙手也無法否認。

愛麗絲抗議：「我不用雙手否認事情。」

紅棋王后說：「沒有人說你這麼做，我說的是，就算你試著這麼做，也做不到。」

白棋王后說：「她現在的心態就是那樣，心裡就是想要否認……只是她也不知道要否認什麼。」

紅棋王后說：「這脾氣真是卑鄙惡劣。」然後是一、兩分鐘讓人不自在的沉默。

後來紅棋王后打破沉默，她對白棋王后說：「我邀請你參加愛麗絲王后今天下午的宴會。」

白棋王后微微一笑，說道：「我也邀請你參加。」

愛麗絲說：「我完全不知道我要舉辦宴會，但如果真的有宴會，我想應該

由我來邀請賓客吧？」

紅棋王后說：「我們已經給過你機會邀請賓客了，但我猜你沒上過幾堂禮儀課吧？」

愛麗絲說：「課堂上教的不是禮儀，而是教算術之類的東西。」

白棋王后問：「那你會加法嗎？一加一加一加一加一加一加一加一加一加一加一等於多少？」

愛麗絲說：「我不知道，我數不清楚有幾個一。」

「她不會加法。」紅棋王后插嘴，「你會減法嗎？八減九等於多少？」

愛麗絲馬上回答：「八減九我不會，但是……」

「她不會減法。」白棋王后說，「你會除法嗎？一條麵包除以一把刀子，答案是什麼？」

「我想……」愛麗絲才剛開口，紅棋王后卻搶著為她回答：「當然是奶油麵包啊。再試一題減法：狗減掉骨頭，還剩什麼？」

愛麗絲想了一下說：「如果我拿走了骨頭，骨頭當然不在了；狗也不在了，因為牠會跑來咬我，我敢說我也不在！」

紅棋王后說：「你覺得沒有東西剩下來？」

「我想答案就是那樣。」

紅棋王后說：「又錯了！狗的脾氣會剩下來。」

「怎麼會……」

紅棋王后大聲說：「哎呀，聽好了！狗會發脾氣，對吧？」

愛麗絲謹慎地回答：「可能吧。」

紅棋王后得意洋洋地大聲說：「那麼你看，就算狗跑掉了，牠發的脾氣會剩下來！」

愛麗絲努力裝作一本正經地說：「狗和脾氣可能走不同的路。」但她忍不住心想：「這究竟在胡說八道什麼啊！」

兩位王后異口同聲地強調：「她完全不會算術！」

愛麗絲不喜歡被人家挑毛病，於是突然問白棋王后：「那你會算術嗎？」

白棋王后倒抽一口氣，閉上眼睛，說道：「如果時間充足的話，我會加法，但我怎麼樣都不會減法！」

紅棋王后說：「你一定認得英文字母吧？」

愛麗絲說：「當然認得。」

白棋王后低聲說：「我也認得，親愛的，我們以後會常常一起唸。我告訴你一個祕密，我看得懂一個字母拼成的單字！那很了不起吧！但是別氣餒，你遲早也會的。」

這時紅棋王后再度開口：「你會回答實用的問題嗎？麵包是怎麼做的？」

愛麗絲急切地大聲說：「我知道答案！先拿些麵粉……」

白棋王后問：「哪裡可以採麵粉？花園還是樹籬？」

愛麗絲解釋：「嗯，根本不是用採的，是用磨的……」

白棋王后說：「田地有幾英畝？你說話不該漏掉這麼多事情。」

紅棋王后焦急地插嘴：「快為她的頭搧搧風！她想了那麼多，一定快發燒了。」因此兩位王后拿著一大把葉子為愛麗絲搧風，直到愛麗絲求她們停下來，她的頭髮被搧得亂七八糟。

「現在她恢復了。」紅棋王后說，「你懂外語嗎？『fiddle-de-dee』的法文怎麼說？」

愛麗絲嚴肅地說：「『fiddle-de-dee』不是英文。」

紅棋王后說：「誰說它是英文？」

愛麗絲心想，這次她終於想到解圍的辦法了。她得意洋洋地大聲說：「如果你告訴我『fiddle-de-dee』是什麼語言，我就跟你說它的法文怎麼說！」

但紅棋王后挺直身子說：「王后從不接受討價還價！」

愛麗絲心想：「我真希望王后永遠別問問題！」

白棋王后焦慮地說：「我們別吵架了。閃電的原因是什麼？」

愛麗絲覺得很有把握，所以果斷地說：「閃電的原因是打雷……」她趕緊

改口：「不對，不對！我的意思是，正好相反。」

紅棋王后說：「現在已經來不及更正了，話一說出口就確定了，後果必須自己承擔。」

白棋王后低著頭，焦慮地一下子握緊手，一下子鬆開手，說道：「這讓我想起一件事，上星期二下了一場很大的雷雨……你懂的，我指的是上一組星期二的其中一天。」

愛麗絲很困惑地說：「在我們的國度，一次就只有一天。」

紅棋王后說：「那樣的做事方法真是粗劣。在這裡，我們大多是兩三個白天或晚上一起過。到了冬天，有時我們一次連過五個晚上……你懂的，這樣比較暖和。」

愛麗絲鼓起勇氣問：「那麼五個晚上連在一起過，比一個晚上溫暖嗎？」

「當然囉，溫暖五倍！」

「但根據相同的道理，應該是寒冷五倍？」

紅棋王后大聲說：「就是這樣！溫暖五倍，也寒冷五倍……就像我比你有錢五倍，也比你聰明五倍！」

愛麗絲嘆了一口氣，放棄爭辯。她心想：「這就像沒有謎底的謎語！」

白棋王后繼續低聲說，看起來更像自言自語：「蛋頭先生也看到了那場雷雨，他來到門口，手裡拿著螺絲錐……」

紅棋王后說：「他想做什麼？」

白棋王后說：「他說他想進來，因為他在找一隻河馬。但那天早上，屋子裡剛好沒有河馬。」

愛麗絲驚訝地問：「屋子裡通常會有河馬嗎？」

白棋王后說：「嗯，只有星期四有。」

愛麗絲說：「我知道蛋頭先生來的目的…他想處罰那些魚，因為……」

白棋王后繼續說：「那場雷雨很大，你想都想不到！（紅棋王后插嘴…『她從來沒在想。』）一部分的屋頂被吹掉，好多雷跑進屋裡，一大團一大團

滾來滾去，撞倒桌子與其他東西。我嚇壞了，甚至想不起來自己的名字！」

愛麗絲心想：「意外發生的時候，我絕對不會試著去想自己叫什麼名字！那有什麼用？」但她沒說出口，擔心會讓可憐的白棋王后難過。

紅棋王后對愛麗絲說：「請陛下一定要原諒她，」她握住白棋王后的一隻手，輕輕撫摸，「她是一番好意，但就是會忍不住說些蠢話，她一向如此。」

白棋王后怯生生地看著愛麗絲，愛麗絲覺得自己應該說些親切的話，但此刻真的一個字也想不出來。

紅棋王后繼續說：「她從沒受過好教養，但她的脾氣好得驚人！拍拍她的頭，你會看到她很高興！」但是愛麗絲根本沒膽拍王后的頭。

「只要對她好一點點，然後用紙捲幫她捲頭髮，她就很高興了。」

白棋王后深深嘆了一口氣，腦袋倚在愛麗絲的肩上，喃喃說著：「我是不是很想睡了？」

紅棋王后說：「她累了，這個可憐的小東西！順一順她的頭髮，把你的睡

帽借給她，再唱一首慢慢的催眠曲給她聽。」

愛麗絲遵從第一個指示，順了順白棋王后的頭髮，然後說：「我身上沒帶睡帽，也不會唱催眠曲。」

紅棋王后說：「那麼就得我來唱了。」她唱了起來：

紅白王后一道去，眾人加上愛麗絲！

等到宴會結束後，我們就要去舞會……

趁著宴會在籌備，抓緊時間先小睡。

白棋王后快快睡，愛麗絲的腿當枕！

紅棋王后接著說：「現在你知道歌詞了。」她將頭靠在愛麗絲另一邊的肩上，「從頭唱一遍給我聽吧，我也睏了。」片刻後，兩位王后皆已酣睡，發出響亮的鼾聲。

愛麗絲大聲說：「現在我該怎麼辦？」她茫然地左看右看，這時兩位王后圓滾滾的頭相繼滑下愛麗絲的肩膀，枕在她的大腿上，像兩團沉甸甸的東西。愛麗絲不耐地繼續說：「一個人必須同時照顧兩位沉睡的王后，我想這種事從來不曾發生！不，整個英國的歷史沒發生過這種事，你懂的，這種事不可能發生，因為同一時期絕不會有兩位王后！你們兩個沉重的傢伙，快點醒來！」但除了輕輕的鼾聲，兩位王后沒有任何回應。

鼾聲越來越清楚，聽起來也越來越

像一首曲子，最後愛麗絲甚至聽出了歌詞。她聽得很專心，就連兩位王后的兩個大腦袋忽然從她腿上消失，她也沒注意到。

愛麗絲站在一扇拱門前，門上寫著「愛麗絲王后」幾個大字，拱門兩側各有一個門鈴拉手，其中一個標示著「訪客鈴」，另一個標示著「僕人鈴」。

愛麗絲心想：「等到這首歌結束，我再來拉鈴，拉……我應該拉哪一個鈴？」門鈴拉手的名稱讓她很困惑，她繼續說：「我不是訪客，也不是僕人，理應有個『王后鈴』啊……」

此時大門開了一條細縫，一隻有著長喙的動物探頭出來一下，說道：「下星期前都不得入內！」接著又砰的一聲關上門。

愛麗絲又是敲門，又是拉鈴，試了許久都沒用。不過，坐在樹下的一隻年邁青蛙最後站了起來，一跛一跛地慢慢地走向愛麗絲。這隻老青蛙穿著亮黃色的衣服，腳上套著一雙大靴子。

老青蛙用低沉沙啞的嗓音輕聲問：「現在是怎麼回事？」

愛麗絲轉過身，準備要找個人出氣。她生氣地問：「負責應門的僕人在哪裡啊？」

老青蛙問：「哪扇門？」

老青蛙說起話來慢吞吞的，愛麗絲聽了氣得幾乎要跺腳，「當然是指這扇門啊！」

老青蛙無神的大眼睛盯著大門看了一會兒，再走近用大拇指抹了一下門，彷彿在檢查油漆會不會剝落，然後回頭望著愛麗絲。

老青蛙說：「回答這扇門？它剛剛問了什麼問題嗎？」牠的聲音很沙啞，愛麗絲幾乎聽不清楚。

她說：「我不懂你的意思。」

老青蛙繼續說：「我剛剛說的是英語，不是嗎？或是你聾了？這扇門問了你什麼問題？」

愛麗絲不耐地說：「它沒問問題，我只是敲門！」

老青蛙喃喃低語：「不該敲它……不該敲它……它會生氣啊，你懂的。」

牠走上前，伸出大腳踢了大門一下，接著一跛一跛地走回樹下，氣喘吁吁地說：「你不惹它，它就不惹你，你懂的。」

這時大門猛地開了，傳出一道尖銳的嗓音唱著歌：

鏡中世界聽分明，我是愛麗絲王后，
我手中握著權杖，頭頂上戴著王冠。
鏡中世界眾子民，歡迎大家來參加，
紅白王后加上我，豐盛饗宴齊同樂。

接著數百個聲音加入合唱：

快將佳釀斟滿杯，速速行動莫遲疑

撒上鈕扣與粗糠，餐桌擺滿眾美食。

貓咪放進咖啡裡，老鼠加進茶水中。

歡迎愛麗絲王后，歡呼三十乘三次！

想知道有誰在數？」不久一切又歸於寂靜，同一道尖銳的嗓音開始唱下一段：

接著響起一陣混亂的歡呼聲。愛麗絲心想：「三十乘三次是九十次，我真

愛麗絲王后宣告，鏡中子民靠過來，

此乃爾等之光榮，觀見王后聽其言。

此乃爾等之殊榮，共享盛宴同品茶。

然後又是大合唱：

杯裡倒滿甜糖蜜，或是斟滿黑墨汁，

喜歡什麼加什麼，開心暢飲樂陶陶。

沙子加進蘋果汁，羊毛摻入葡萄酒。

歡迎愛麗絲王后，歡呼九十乘九次！

「九十乘九次！」愛麗絲絕望地重複說了一遍，「噢，那數不完的！我最好馬上進去……」說完就走了進去，她一現身，全場立刻一片死寂。

愛麗絲走進寬敞的大廳裡，緊張地瞥了一眼長桌，注意到賓客約有五十位，這些賓客形形色色，有些是動物，有些是鳥兒，甚至還有幾朵鮮花。愛麗絲心想：「真高興，我不用邀請他們，他們就來了，不然我還不知道該邀請哪些賓客才好！」

主位有三張椅子，紅棋王后與白棋王后各坐一張，但中間那張是空的。愛麗絲坐在那張空椅上，四周一片安靜，她覺得很不自在，希望有人開口說話。

最後紅棋王后開口：「你已經錯過湯品和魚肉了。」她吩咐：「上羊腿！」侍者端了一大塊帶骨羊腿，放在愛麗絲面前。愛麗絲焦慮地望著羊腿，因為她從沒切過這麼大塊的肉。

紅棋王后說：「你看起來有點害羞，我為你介紹這隻羊腿吧。愛麗絲，這是羊腿；羊腿，這是愛麗絲。」盤子裡的羊腿站了起來，向愛麗絲微微鞠躬，愛麗絲還禮，她不知道自己該覺得害怕或好笑。

她拿起刀叉，輪流看著兩位王后說：

「我為你們切一片羊腿肉好嗎？」

紅棋王后堅決地說：「當然不好。你已經認識對方了，切它實在很失禮。撤下羊腿！」

侍者撤走羊腿，換上一大個葡萄乾布丁。

愛麗絲趕緊說：「拜託，別介紹我認識布丁，否則我們什麼都吃不到了。

我切點布丁給你們好嗎？」

但紅棋王后繃著臉低吼：「布丁，這是愛麗絲；愛麗絲，這是布丁。撤下布丁！」愛麗絲還來不及還禮，侍者就迅速端走了布丁。

然而，愛麗絲不明白為何只有紅棋王后可以下命令，所以她試著大喊：

「侍者！把布丁端回來！」布丁立刻再度出現在桌上，就像變魔術一樣。這個布丁很大，愛麗絲忍不住覺得有些害羞，就像剛剛面對羊腿時一樣，但她努力克服羞怯，切了一片布丁給紅棋王后。

布丁說：「真是無禮！如果我從你身上切一片下來，你會有什麼感覺？」

布丁的聲音厚實又油膩，愛麗絲想不出回答的話，只能坐在那兒盯著它，倒抽一口氣。

紅棋王后說：「你快說話啊！全讓布丁自個兒說話，這樣太荒謬了！」

愛麗絲說：「你知道嗎？今天很多人唸詩給我聽。」她一開口就發現全場

立刻陷入死寂，所有眼睛都盯著她，這讓她有點害怕，「我覺得奇怪的是……

每首詩都多多少少跟魚有關。你知不知道為什麼這裡的人都這麼喜歡魚啊？」

愛麗絲對著紅棋王后說這番話，紅棋王后的回答有點答非所問，她湊近愛麗絲的耳邊，一本正經的慢慢說：「說到魚嘛，白棋王后陛下知道一個可愛謎語……它寫成一首詩……也跟魚有關。請她唸如何？」

「承蒙紅棋王后陛下的好意，特意提到這首詩。」白棋王后對著愛麗絲的另一隻耳朵低聲說，她的聲音聽起來像鴿子的咕咕聲，「這是難得的樂事！要我唸嗎？」

愛麗絲彬彬有禮地回答：「請。」

白棋王后開心地笑了出來，摸摸愛麗絲的臉頰，接著開始唸：

「首先得抓魚。」

輕而易舉，小孩子都抓得到。

「接著得買魚。」

「輕而易舉，一塊錢就買得到。」

「再來要煮魚。」

「輕而易舉，一分鐘就能煮熟。」

「將魚擺在盤子裡。」

「輕而易舉，因為魚已在盤裡。」

「拿來讓我嚐！」

「輕而易舉，盤子輕鬆擺上桌。」

「快掀開盤蓋！」

談何容易，恐怕我沒那能耐。

盤蓋緊黏如膠水，

盤子蓋子分不開，魚兒擺在盤中央。

何者較簡單：

打開盤蓋，或是解開謎底？

紅棋王后：「你花一分鐘想一想，再猜一猜。」她用最大的嗓門尖聲說：

「在此同時，我們舉杯祝你身體健康……敬祝愛麗絲王后身體健康！」所有的

賓客立刻舉杯喝酒，但他們喝酒的方式非常古怪：有的把酒杯當成了滅燭器，

倒扣在頭頂，再舔乾流到臉上的酒；有的弄翻酒瓶，等到酒液流到桌子邊緣再

湊過去喝。其中三位賓客（看起來像袋鼠）爬進烤羊肉的盤子裡，急切地舔起

肉汁，愛麗絲心想：「簡直像擠在飼料槽旁邊的豬！」

紅棋王后皺著眉對愛麗絲說：「你應該簡單說幾句感謝的話。」

愛麗絲很聽話，起身準備說話，但有點怯場。白棋王后低聲說：「我們一

定會撐住你。」

愛麗絲低聲回答：「十分感謝，但我不需要你們的支持也能講得很好。」

紅棋王后堅決地說：「絕對不可能。」所以愛麗絲只好優雅地接受。

（愛麗絲後來跟姐姐講述宴會的過程：「她們真的很用力擠我！根本想把我擠扁！」）

事實上，愛麗絲說話的時候，真的很難站穩：兩位王后一左一右用力擠她，幾乎把她擠到空中。愛麗絲才開口說：「我起身感謝……」時，身體就上升了好幾公分，不過她抓住了桌子邊緣，好不容易把自己再拉下來。

（根據愛麗絲後來的描述）接著，各種事情瞬間發生：所有蠟燭向上長到天花板，看起來像頂端燃著煙火的一大片燈心草；每個酒瓶都抓了兩個盤子，急忙裝在身上當翅膀，還拿叉子當腳，拍動翅膀四處亂走，愛麗絲心想：「它們還看起來真像鳥。」

白棋王后雙手抓著愛麗絲的頭髮，尖叫著：「保重啊！有事要發生了！」愛麗絲處在這麼可怕的混亂場面裡，努力想著這些事。

此時愛麗絲聽到身旁傳來沙啞的笑聲，她轉頭看看白棋王后發生了什麼事，但坐在椅子上的不是王后，而是羊腿。湯碗裡傳來大喊的聲音：「我在這

裡！」愛麗絲再度轉頭，正好看到白棋王后那張和善的大臉在湯碗邊緣對她咧嘴一笑，接著消失在湯裡。

情況緊急，刻不容緩，已經有好幾位賓客躺在盤子裡，餐桌的湯勺走向愛麗絲的座位，還不耐煩地揮手示意她別擋路。

愛麗絲大喊：「我再也受不了了！」她跳起來，雙手抓著桌巾用力一拉，盤子、碟子、賓客、蠟燭統統摔在地上，疊成一堆。

認爲這場惡作劇的罪魁禍首是紅棋王后，她怒氣沖沖地轉身罵王后：「至於你，」但王后已經不坐在愛麗絲身邊，而是忽然縮成小洋娃娃的大小，正在餐桌上高興地跑來跑去，追著自己背後飄揚的披肩繞圈圈。

若是其他時候，愛麗絲可能會感到驚訝，但現在她已經氣壞了，對任何事情都不感驚訝了。她又說了一次：「至於你，」那個小傢伙正要跳過剛剛降落在桌上的一支酒瓶，愛麗絲一把抓住她，說道：「我要狠狠搖晃你，把你搖成一隻小貓咪，我一定要！」

如果有人介紹羊腿給你認識，羊腿也跟你打了招呼，那你還會切下羊腿來吃嗎？

第十章　搖晃

愛麗絲一邊說，一邊從餐桌上抓起紅棋王后，用盡全力來回搖晃。

紅棋王后沒反抗，但她的臉越來越小，眼睛越來越大還變成綠色。愛麗絲繼續搖晃，她變得越來越矮……越來越胖……越來越軟……越來越圓……然後……

第十一章 醒來

……她真的變成一隻小貓了。

第十二章 誰做的夢？

愛麗絲揉揉眼睛，恭恭敬敬又有些嚴厲對小貓說：「紅棋王后陛下，你不該這麼大聲發出呼嚕呼嚕聲，我做了一個好夢，你竟然把我吵醒了！凱蒂啊，你跟著我一起去了鏡中世界，親愛的，你知道嗎？」

（愛麗絲曾說過）小貓咪有個麻煩的習慣，那就是不管你對牠們說什麼，牠們永遠只會呼嚕回應。愛麗絲說：「如果牠們發出呼嚕聲表示『是』，喵喵叫表示『不是』，或是有類似規則的話，我們就可以聊天了！但如果對方總是講同一句話，怎麼能聊得下去呢？」

這時小貓咪只是發出呼嚕聲，根本猜不出牠在表達「是」或者「不是」。

所以愛麗絲在桌上的棋子裡尋找，直到找出紅棋王后，接著跪在壁爐前的

地毯上，把紅棋王后與小貓咪
擺好，讓她們面對面。愛麗絲
得意洋洋地拍手，大聲說：

「好了，凱蒂！快承認你剛剛
變成紅棋王后！」

（後來愛麗絲對姐姐解
釋：「但凱蒂不願意看著紅棋
王后，牠把頭轉開，假裝沒看
見，但牠看起來有點難為情，
所以我覺得牠一定當過紅棋
王后。」）

愛麗絲高興地笑著大喊：

「親愛的，坐直一點！你可以

一邊想著該怎麼……怎麼發出呼嚕聲，一邊行屈膝禮，這樣能節省時間，記住了！」她把小貓咪抱起來輕輕吻一下，「這是為了紀念你當過紅棋王后！」

愛麗絲轉頭看著小白貓，小白貓仍耐心地讓貓媽媽洗臉，「我的寶貝雪兒！黛娜何時才會幫白棋王后陛下洗完臉呢？這一定是你在我的夢裡很邋遢的原因。黛娜！你知不知道你擦洗的是白棋王后？說真的，你真是大不敬！

愛麗絲舒舒服服趴在地毯上，一手撐著下巴，看著眼前這些貓咪，繼續嘰嘰喳喳地說：「我真想知道黛娜變成了什麼？黛娜，告訴我，你是不是變成蛋頭先生了？我覺得你應該是變成他了，但你最好先別告訴你朋友，因為我還不是很確定。」

「喔對了，凱蒂，要是你真的跟我一起出現在我的夢裡，有件事你會很喜歡……我聽了很多首詩，每首都跟魚有關！明天早上你真的有耳福了！你一邊吃早餐，我一邊唸那首《海象與木匠》給你聽，親愛的，你就能假裝你吃的是牡蠣！」

「好了，凱蒂，我們來想一想到底是誰夢到這一切？親愛的，這是嚴肅的問題，你不該一直那樣舔爪子，彷彿今天早上黛娜沒幫你洗臉似的。你知道的，做夢的人一定是我或紅棋國王，當然啦，他在我的夢境裡……但我也在他的夢境裡！凱蒂，做夢的人是紅棋國王嗎？親愛的，你是他的王后，你應該知道吧……噢，凱蒂，拜託先幫我解答！等一下再舔你的爪子！」那隻不聽話的小貓咪卻只是開始舔另一隻爪子，假裝沒聽到這個問題。

你覺得這究竟是誰做的夢呢？

七月日暮映晚霞，

夕陽下一葉扁舟，

如夢似幻任漂流……

三個孩童傍身邊，

眼神祈求耳拉長，

盼望聽個小故事……

秋日霜寒七月換，
燦爛晚霞早已淡，
回聲模糊記憶散。

恬念愛麗絲身影，
穹蒼之下伊漫行，
清醒時刻不復見。

孩童渴望聽故事，
眼神祈求耳拉長，
親暱依偎在身旁。

夢裡逍遙奇境裡，
夢裡樂遊時光逝，
夢裡歡笑夏日過。

依然沿溪任漂流，
小舟緩行霞光中，
人生豈非夢一場？

想一想

在愛麗絲夢中遇見的所有角色裡，你喜歡的有哪些？不喜歡的又有哪些？為什麼？

愛麗絲鏡中奇遇

Through the Looking-Glass

中英雙語版

Lewis Carroll

Illustrated by John Tenniel

（原版約翰‧田尼爾復刻手繪插圖）

晨星出版

THROUGH THE LOOKING-GLASS

CONTENTS

01 ╱ Looking-Glass House ··················· *006*

02 ╱ The Garden of Live Flowers ············ *026*

03 ╱ Looking-Glass Insects ··················· *041*

04 ╱ Tweedledum and Tweedledee ········· *056*

05 ╱ Wool and Water ························· *076*

06 ╱ Humpty Dumpty ························· *093*

07 ╱ The Lion and the Unicorn ··············· *111*

08 ╱ 'It's My Own Invention' ············ *126*

09 ╱ Queen Alice ························· *148*

10 ╱ Shaking ···························· *170*

11 ╱ Waking ···························· *171*

12 ╱ Which Dreamed it? ···················· *172*

01 /

Looking-Glass House

One thing was certain, that the *white* kitten had had nothing to do with it:—it was the black kitten's fault entirely. For the white kitten had been having its face washed by the old cat for the last quarter of an hour (and bearing it pretty well, considering); so you see that it *couldn't* have had any hand in the mischief.

The way Dinah washed her children's faces was this: first she held the poor thing down by its ear with one paw, and then with the other paw she rubbed its face all over, the wrong way, beginning at the nose: and just now, as I said, she was hard at work on the white kitten, which was lying quite still and trying to purr—no doubt feeling that it was all meant for its good.

But the black kitten had been finished with earlier in the afternoon, and so, while Alice was sitting curled up in a corner of the great arm-chair, half talking to herself and half asleep, the kitten had been having a grand game of romps with the ball of worsted Alice had been trying to

wind up, and had been rolling it up and down till it had all come undone again; and there it was, spread over the hearth-rug, all knots and tangles, with the kitten running after its own tail in the middle.

'Oh, you wicked little thing!' cried Alice, catching up the kitten, and giving it a little kiss to make it understand that it was in disgrace. 'Really, Dinah ought to have taught you better manners! You *ought*, Dinah, you know you ought!' she added, looking reproachfully at the old cat, and

reproachfully [rɪˈprotʃfəlɪ] *adv* 責備地

speaking in as cross a voice as she could manage—and then she scrambled back into the arm-chair, taking the kitten and the worsted with her, and began winding up the ball again. But she didn't get on very fast, as she was talking all the time, sometimes to the kitten, and sometimes to herself. Kitty sat very demurely on her knee, pretending to watch the progress of the winding, and now and then putting out one paw and gently touching the ball, as if it would be glad to help, if it might.

'Do you know what to-morrow is, Kitty?' Alice began. 'You'd have guessed if you'd been up in the window with me—only Dinah was making you tidy, so you couldn't. I was watching the boys getting in sticks for the bonfire—and it wants plenty of sticks, Kitty! Only it got so cold, and it snowed so, they had to leave off. Never mind, Kitty, we'll go and see the bonfire to-morrow.' Here Alice wound two or three turns of the worsted round the kitten's neck, just to see how it would look: this led to a scramble, in which the ball rolled down upon the floor, and yards and yards of it got unwound again.

'Do you know, I was so angry, Kitty,' Alice went on as soon as they were comfortably settled again, 'when I saw

demurely [dɪˈmjʊrlɪ] **adv** 裝成端莊地；認真地

all the mischief you had been doing, I was very nearly opening the window, and putting you out into the snow! And you'd have deserved it, you little mischievous darling! What have you got to say for yourself? Now don't interrupt me!' she went on, holding up one finger. 'I'm going to tell you all your faults. Number one: you squeaked twice while Dinah was washing your face this morning. Now you can't deny it, Kitty: I heard you! What's that you say?' (pretending that the kitten was speaking.) 'Her paw went into your eye? Well, that's *your* fault, for keeping your eyes open—if you'd shut them tight up, it wouldn't have happened. Now don't make any more excuses, but listen! Number two: you pulled Snowdrop away by the tail just as I had put down the saucer of milk before her! What, you were thirsty, were you? How do you know she wasn't thirsty too? Now for number three: you unwound every bit of the worsted while I wasn't looking!

'That's three faults, Kitty, and you've not been punished for any of them yet. You know I'm saving up all your punishments for Wednesday week—Suppose they had saved up all *mypunishments*!' she went on, talking more to herself than the kitten. 'What *would* they do at the end of a year? I should be sent to prison, I suppose, when the day came. Or—let me see—suppose each punishment was to be going without a dinner: then, when

the miserable day came, I should have to go without fifty dinners at once! Well, I shouldn't mind *that* much! I'd far rather go without them than eat them!

'Do you hear the snow against the window-panes, Kitty? How nice and soft it sounds! Just as if some one was kissing the window all over outside. I wonder if the snow *loves* the trees and fields, that it kisses them so gently? And then it covers them up snug, you know, with a white quilt; and perhaps it says, "Go to sleep, darlings, till the summer comes again." And when they wake up in the summer, Kitty, they dress themselves all in green, and dance about—whenever the wind blows—oh, that's very pretty!' cried Alice, dropping the ball of worsted to clap her hands. 'And I do so *wish* it was true! I'm sure the woods look sleepy in the autumn, when the leaves are getting brown.

'Kitty, can you play chess? Now, don't smile, my dear, I'm asking it seriously. Because, when we were playing just now, you watched just as if you understood it: and when I said "Check!" you purred! Well, it *was* a nice check, Kitty, and really I might have won, if it hadn't been for that nasty Knight, that came wiggling down among my pieces. Kitty, dear, let's pretend—' And here I wish I could tell you half the things Alice used to say, beginning with her favourite phrase 'Let's pretend.' She had had quite a long argument with her sister only the day before—all because

Alice had begun with 'Let's pretend we're kings and queens;' and her sister, who liked being very exact, had argued that they couldn't, because there were only two of them, and Alice had been reduced at last to say, 'Well, *you* can be one of them then, and *I'll* be all the rest.' And once she had really frightened her old nurse by shouting suddenly in her ear, 'Nurse! Do let's pretend that I'm a hungry hyaena, and you're a bone.'

But this is taking us away from Alice's speech to the kitten. 'Let's pretend that you're the Red Queen, Kitty! Do you know, I think if you sat up and folded your arms, you'd look exactly like her. Now do try, there's a dear!' And Alice got the Red Queen off the table, and set it up before the kitten as a model for it to imitate: however, the thing didn't succeed, principally, Alice said, because the kitten wouldn't fold its arms properly. So, to punish it, she held it up to the Looking-glass, that it might see how sulky it was—'and if you're not good directly,' she added, 'I'll put you through into Looking-glass House. How would you like *that?*'

'Now, if you'll only attend, Kitty, and not talk so much, I'll tell you all my ideas about Looking-glass House.

sulky ['sʌlkɪ] *adj* 生氣的，繃著臉的

First, there's the room you can see through the glass—that's just the same as our drawing room, only the things go the other way. I can see all of it when I get upon a chair—all but the bit behind the fireplace. Oh! I do so wish I could see *that* bit! I want so much to know whether they've a fire in the winter: you never *can* tell, you know, unless our fire smokes, and then smoke comes up in that room too—but that may be only pretence, just to make it look as if they had a fire. Well then, the books are something like our books, only the words go the wrong way; I know that, because I've held up one of our books to the glass, and then they hold up one in the other room.

'How would you like to live in Looking-glass House, Kitty? I wonder if they'd give you milk in there? Perhaps Looking-glass milk isn't good to drink—But oh, Kitty! now we come to the passage. You can just see a little *peep* of the passage in Looking-glass House, if you leave the door of our drawing-room wide open: and it's very like our passage as far as you can see, only you know it may be quite different on beyond. Oh, Kitty! how nice it would be if we could only get through into Looking-glass House! I'm sure it's got, oh! such beautiful things in it! Let's pretend there's a way of getting through into it, somehow, Kitty. Let's pretend the glass has got all soft like gauze, so that we can get through. Why, it's turning into a sort of mist now, I declare! It'll be easy enough to get through—' She was up

on the chimney-piece while she said this, though she hardly knew how she had got there. And certainly the glass *was* beginning to melt away, just like a bright silvery mist.

In another moment Alice was through the glass, and had jumped lightly down into the Looking-glass room. The very first thing she did was to look whether there was a fire in the fireplace, and she was quite pleased to find that there was a real one, blazing away as brightly as the

one she had left behind. 'So I shall be as warm here as I was in the old room,' thought Alice: 'warmer, in fact, because there'll be no one here to scold me away from the fire. Oh, what fun it'll be, when they see me through the glass in here, and can't get at me!'

Then she began looking about, and noticed that what could be seen from the old room was quite common and uninteresting, but that all the rest was as different as

possible. For instance, the pictures on the wall next the fire seemed to be all alive, and the very clock on the chimney-piece (you know you can only see the back of it in the Looking-glass) had got the face of a little old man, and grinned at her.

'They don't keep this room so tidy as the other,' Alice thought to herself, as she noticed several of the chessmen down in the hearth among the cinders: but in another moment, with a little 'Oh!' of surprise, she was down on her hands and knees watching them. The chessmen were walking about, two and two!

'Here are the Red King and the Red Queen,' Alice said (in a whisper, for fear of frightening them), 'and there

are the White King and the White Queen sitting on the edge of the shovel—and here are two castles walking arm in arm—I don't think they can hear me,' she went on, as she put her head closer down, 'and I'm nearly sure they can't see me. I feel somehow as if I were invisible—'

Here something began squeaking on the table behind Alice, and made her turn her head just in time to see one of the White Pawns roll over and begin kicking: she watched it with great curiosity to see what would happen next.

'It is the voice of my child!' the White Queen cried out as she rushed past the King, so violently that she knocked him over among the cinders. 'My precious Lily! My imperial kitten!' and she began scrambling wildly up the side of the fender.

'Imperial fiddlestick!' said the King, rubbing his nose, which had been hurt by the fall. He had a right to be a *little* annoyed with the Queen, for he was covered with ashes from head to foot.

Alice was very anxious to be of use, and, as the poor little Lily was nearly screaming herself into a fit, she hastily picked up the Queen and set her on the table by the side of her noisy little daughter.

imperial [ɪmˈpɪrɪəl] *adj* 女皇的；最高（權力）的

The Queen gasped, and sat down: the rapid journey through the air had quite taken away her breath and for a minute or two she could do nothing but hug the little Lily in silence. As soon as she had recovered her breath a little, she called out to the White King, who was sitting sulkily among the ashes, 'Mind the volcano!'

'What volcano?' said the King, looking up anxiously into the fire, as if he thought that was the most likely place to find one.

'Blew—me—up,' panted the Queen, who was still a little out of breath. 'Mind you come up—the regular way—don't get blown up!'

Alice watched the White King as he slowly struggled up from bar to bar, till at last she said, 'Why, you'll be hours and hours getting to the table, at that rate. I'd far better help you, hadn't I?' But the King took no notice of the question: it was quite clear that he could neither hear her nor see her.

So Alice picked him up very gently, and lifted him across more slowly than she had lifted the Queen, that she mightn't

take his breath away: but, before she put him on the table, she thought she might as well dust him a little, he was so covered with ashes.

She said afterwards that she had never seen in all her life such a face as the King made, when he found himself held in the air by an invisible hand, and being dusted: he was far too much astonished to cry out, but his eyes and his mouth went on getting larger and larger, and rounder and rounder, till her hand shook so with laughing that she nearly let him drop upon the floor.

'Oh! *please* don't make such faces, my dear!' she cried out, quite forgetting that the King couldn't hear her. 'You make me laugh so that I can hardly hold you! And don't keep your mouth so wide open! All the ashes will get into it—there, now I think you're tidy enough!' she added, as she smoothed his hair, and set him upon the table near the Queen.

The King immediately fell flat on his back, and lay perfectly still: and Alice was a little alarmed at what she had done, and went round the room to see if she could find any water to throw over him. However, she could find nothing but a bottle of ink, and when she got back

astonished [əˈstɑnɪʃt] *adj* 驚訝的;驚愕的

with it she found he had recovered, and he and the Queen were talking together in a frightened whisper—so low, that Alice could hardly hear what they said.

The King was saying, 'I assure, you my dear, I turned cold to the very ends of my whiskers!'

To which the Queen replied, 'You haven't got any whiskers.'

'The horror of that moment,' the King went on, 'I shall never, *never* forget!'

'You will, though,' the Queen said, 'if you don't make a memorandum of it.'

Alice looked on with great interest as the King took an enormous memorandum-book out of his pocket, and began writing. A sudden thought struck her, and she took hold of the end of the pencil, which came some way over his shoulder, and began writing for him.

The poor King looked puzzled and unhappy, and struggled with the pencil for some time without saying anything; but Alice was too strong for him, and at last he panted out, 'My dear! I really *must* get a thinner pencil. I can't manage this one a bit; it writes all manner of things that I don't intend—'

'What manner of things?' said the Queen, looking over the book (in which Alice had put 'The White Knight is sliding down the poker. He balances very badly') 'That's not a memorandum of *your* feelings!'

There was a book lying near Alice on the table, and while she sat watching the White King (for she was still a little anxious about him, and had the ink all ready to throw over him, in case he fainted again), she turned over the leaves, to find some part that she could read, '—for it's all in some language I don't know,' she said to herself.

It was like this.

YKCOWREBBAJ

sevot yhtils eht dna,gillirb sawT'
ebaw eht ni elbmig dna eryg diD
,sevogorob eht erew ysmim llA
.ebargtuo shtar emom eht dnA

She puzzled over this for some time, but at last a bright thought struck her. 'Why, it's a Looking-glass book, of course! And if I hold it up to a glass, the words will all go the right way again.'

This was the poem that Alice read.

JABBERWOCKY

'Twas brillig, and the slithy toves
Did gyre and gimble in the wabe;
All mimsy were the borogoves,
And the mome raths outgrabe.

'Beware the Jabberwock, my son!
The jaws that bite, the claws that catch!
Beware the Jubjub bird, and shun
The frumious Bandersnatch!'

He took his vorpal sword in hand:
Long time the manxome foe he sought—
So rested he by the Tumtum tree,
And stood awhile in thought.

And as in uffish thought he stood,
The Jabberwock, with eyes of flame,
Came whiffling through the tulgey wood,
And burbled as it came!

One, two! One, two! And through and through
The vorpal blade went snicker-snack!
He left it dead, and with its head
He went galumphing back.

'And hast thou slain the Jabberwock?
Come to my arms, my beamish boy!
O frabjous day! Callooh! Callay!'
He chortled *in his joy.*

'Twas brillig, and the slithy toves
Did gyre and gimble in the wabe;
All mimsy were the borogoves,
And the mome raths outgrabe.

'It seems very pretty,' she said when she had finished it, 'but it's *rather* hard to understand!' (You see she didn't like to confess, ever to herself, that she couldn't make it out at all.) 'Somehow it seems to fill my head with ideas— only I don't exactly know what they are! However, *somebody* killed *something*: that's clear, at any rate—'

'But oh!' thought Alice, suddenly jumping up, 'if I don't make haste I shall have to go back through the

chortle ['tʃɔrtl] **v** 得意地咯咯笑；哈哈大笑

Looking-glass, before I've seen what the rest of the house is like! Let's have a look at the garden first!' She was out of the room in a moment, and ran down stairs—or, at least, it wasn't exactly running, but a new invention of hers for getting down stairs quickly and easily, as Alice said to herself. She just kept the tips of her fingers on the hand-rail, and floated gently down without even touching the stairs with her feet; then she floated on through the hall, and would have gone straight out at the door in the same way, if she hadn't caught hold of the door-post. She was getting a little giddy with so much floating in the air, and was rather glad to find herself walking again in the natural way.

giddy [ˈgɪdɪ] *adj* 暈眩的，眼花的

The Garden of Live Flowers

'I should see the garden far better,' said Alice to herself, 'if I could get to the top of that hill: and here's a path that leads straight to it—at least, no, it doesn't do

that—' (after going a few yards along the path, and turning several sharp corners), 'but I suppose it will at last. But how curiously it twists! It's more like a corkscrew than a path! Well, *this* turn goes to the hill, I suppose—no, it doesn't! This goes straight back to the house! Well then, I'll try it the other way.'

And so she did: wandering up and down, and trying turn after turn, but always coming back to the house, do what she would. Indeed, once, when she turned a corner rather more quickly than usual, she ran against it before she could stop herself.

'It's no use talking about it,' Alice said, looking up at the house and pretending it was arguing with her. 'I'm *not* going in again yet. I know I should have to get through the Looking-glass again—back into the old room—and there'd be an end of all my adventures!'

So, resolutely turning her back upon the house, she set out once more down the path, determined to keep straight on till she got to the hill. For a few minutes all went on well, and she was just saying, 'I really *shall* do it this time—' when the path gave a sudden twist and shook itself (as she described it afterwards), and the next

resolutely [ˈrɛzəˌlutlɪ] *adv* 堅決地；毅然地

moment she found herself actually walking in at the door.

'Oh, it's too bad!' she cried. 'I never saw such a house for getting in the way! Never!'

However, there was the hill full in sight, so there was nothing to be done but start again. This time she came upon a large flower-bed, with a border of daisies, and a willow-tree growing in the middle.

'O Tiger-lily,' said Alice, addressing herself to one that was waving gracefully about in the wind, 'I *wish* you could talk!'

'We *can* talk,' said the Tiger-lily: 'when there's anybody worth talking to.'

Alice was so astonished that she could not speak for a minute: it quite seemed to take her breath away. At length, as the Tiger-lily only went on waving about, she spoke again, in a timid voice—almost in a whisper. 'And can *all* the flowers talk?'

'As well as *you* can,' said the Tiger-lily. 'And a great deal louder.'

'It isn't manners for us to begin, you know,' said the Rose, 'and I really was wondering when you'd speak! Said I to myself, "Her face has got *some* sense in it, though it's not a clever one!" Still, you're the right colour, and that goes a long way.'

'I don't care about the colour,' the Tiger-lily remarked. 'If only her petals curled up a little more, she'd be all right.'

Alice didn't like being criticised, so she began asking questions. 'Aren't you sometimes frightened at being planted out here, with nobody to take care of you?'

'There's the tree in the middle,' said the Rose: 'what else is it good for?'

'But what could it do, if any danger came?' Alice asked.

'It says "Bough-wough!"' cried a Daisy: 'that's why its branches are called boughs!'

'Didn't you know *that*?' cried another Daisy, and here they all began shouting together, till the air seemed quite full of little shrill voices. 'Silence, every one of you!' cried the Tiger-lily, waving itself passionately from side to side, and trembling with excitement. 'They know I can't get at them!' it panted, bending its quivering head towards Alice, 'or they wouldn't dare to do it!'

'Never mind!' Alice said in a soothing tone, and stooping down to the daisies, who were just beginning again, she whispered, 'If you don't hold your tongues, I'll pick you!'

There was silence in a moment, and several of the pink daisies turned white.

'That's right!' said the Tiger-lily. 'The daisies are worst of all. When one speaks, they all begin together, and it's enough to make one wither to hear the way they go on!'

'How is it you can all talk so nicely?' Alice said,

hoping to get it into a better temper by a compliment. 'I've been in many gardens before, but none of the flowers could talk.'

'Put your hand down, and feel the ground,' said the Tiger-lily. 'Then you'll know why.'

Alice did so. 'It's very hard,' she said, 'but I don't see what that has to do with it.'

'In most gardens,' the Tiger-lily said, 'they make the beds too soft—so that the flowers are always asleep.'

This sounded a very good reason, and Alice was quite pleased to know it. 'I never thought of that before!' she said.

'It's *my* opinion that you never think *at all*,' the Rose said in a rather severe tone.

'I never saw anybody that looked stupider,' a Violet said, so suddenly, that Alice quite jumped; for it hadn't spoken before.

'Hold *your* tongue!' cried the Tiger-lily. 'As if *you* ever saw anybody! You keep your head under the leaves, and snore away there, till you know no more what's going on in the world, than if you were a bud!'

'Are there any more people in the garden besides me?' Alice said, not choosing to notice the Rose's last remark.

'There's one other flower in the garden that can move about like you,' said the Rose. 'I wonder how you do it—' ('You're always wondering,' said the Tiger-lily), 'but she's

more bushy than you are.'

'Is she like me?' Alice asked eagerly, for the thought crossed her mind, 'There's another little girl in the garden, somewhere!'

'Well, she has the same awkward shape as you,' the Rose said, 'but she's redder—and her petals are shorter, I think.'

'Her petals are done up close, almost like a dahlia,' the Tiger-lily interrupted: 'not tumbled about anyhow, like yours.'

'But that's not *your* fault,' the Rose added kindly: 'you're beginning to fade, you know—and then one can't help one's petals getting a little untidy.'

Alice didn't like this idea at all: so, to change the subject, she asked 'Does she ever come out here?'

'I daresay you'll see her soon,' said the Rose. 'She's one of the thorny kind.'

'Where does she wear the thorns?' Alice asked with some curiosity.

'Why all round her head, of course,' the Rose replied. 'I was wondering *you* hadn't got some too. I thought it was the regular rule.'

'She's coming!' cried the Larkspur. 'I hear her footstep, thump, thump, thump, along the gravel-walk!'

Alice looked round eagerly, and found that it was the Red Queen. 'She's grown a good deal!' was her first

remark. She had indeed: when Alice first found her in the ashes, she had been only three inches high—and here she was, half a head taller than Alice herself!

'It's the fresh air that does it,' said the Rose: 'wonderfully fine air it is, out here.'

'I think I'll go and meet her,' said Alice, for, though the flowers were interesting enough, she felt that it would be far grander to have a talk with a real Queen.

'You can't possibly do that,' said the Rose: '*I* should advise you to walk the other way.'

This sounded nonsense to Alice, so she said nothing, but set off at once towards the Red Queen. To her surprise, she lost sight of her in a moment, and found herself walking in at the front-door again.

A little provoked, she drew back, and after looking everywhere for the queen (whom she spied out at last, a long way off), she thought she would try the plan, this time, of walking in the opposite direction.

It succeeded beautifully. She had not been walking a minute before she found herself face to face with the Red Queen, and full in sight of the hill she had been so long aiming at.

provoked [prə'vokt] *adj* 被激怒的，受到挑釁的

'Where do you come from?' said the Red Queen. 'And where are you going? Look up, speak nicely, and don't twiddle your fingers all the time.'

Alice attended to all these directions, and explained, as well as she could, that she had lost her way.

'I don't know what you mean by *your* way,' said the Queen: 'all the ways about here belong to *me*—but why

did you come out here at all?' she added in a kinder tone. 'Curtsey while you're thinking what to say, it saves time.'

Alice wondered a little at this, but she was too much in awe of the Queen to disbelieve it. 'I'll try it when I go home,' she thought to herself, 'the next time I'm a little late for dinner.'

'It's time for you to answer now,' the Queen said, looking at her watch: 'open your mouth a *little* wider when you speak, and always say "your Majesty."'

'I only wanted to see what the garden was like, your Majesty—'

'That's right,' said the Queen, patting her on the head, which Alice didn't like at all, 'though, when you say "garden,"—*I've* seen gardens, compared with which this would be a wilderness.'

Alice didn't dare to argue the point, but went on: '—and I thought I'd try and find my way to the top of that hill—'

'When you say "hill,"' the Queen interrupted, '*I* could show you hills, in comparison with which you'd call that a valley.'

'No, I shouldn't,' said Alice, surprised into contradicting

contradict [ˌkɑntrəˈdɪkt] ⓥ 反駁；提出論據反對

her at last: 'a hill *can't* be a valley, you know. That would be nonsense—'

The Red Queen shook her head, 'You may call it "nonsense" if you like,' she said, 'but *I've* heard nonsense, compared with which that would be as sensible as a dictionary!'

Alice curtseyed again, as she was afraid from the Queen's tone that she was a *little* offended: and they walked on in silence till they got to the top of the little hill.

For some minutes Alice stood without speaking, looking out in all directions over the country—and a most curious country it was. There were a number of tiny little brooks running straight across it from side to side, and the ground between was divided up into squares by a number of little green hedges, that reached from brook to brook.

'I declare it's marked out just like a large chessboard!' Alice said at last. 'There ought to be some men moving about somewhere—and so there are!' She added in a tone of delight, and her heart began to beat quick with excitement as she went on. 'It's a great huge game of chess that's being played—all over the world—if this *is* the world at all, you know. Oh, what fun it is! How I *wish* I was one of them! I wouldn't mind being a Pawn, if only I might join—though of course I should *like* to be a Queen, best.'

She glanced rather shyly at the real Queen as she said this, but her companion only smiled pleasantly, and said, 'That's easily managed. You can be the White Queen's Pawn, if you like, as Lily's too young to play; and you're in the Second Square to begin with: when you get to the Eighth Square you'll be a Queen—' Just at this moment, somehow or other, they began to run.

Alice never could quite make out, in thinking it over afterwards, how it was that they began: all she remembers is, that they were running hand in hand, and the Queen went so fast that it was all she could do to keep up with her: and still the Queen kept crying 'Faster! Faster!' but Alice felt she *could not* go faster, though she had not breath left to say so.

The most curious part of the thing was, that the trees and the other things round them never changed their places at all: however fast they went, they never seemed to pass anything. 'I wonder if all the things move along with us?' thought poor puzzled Alice. And the Queen seemed to guess her thoughts, for she cried, 'Faster! Don't try to talk!'

Not that Alice had any idea of doing *that*. She felt as if she would never be able to talk again, she was getting so much out of breath: and still the Queen cried 'Faster! Faster!' and dragged her along. 'Are we nearly there?' Alice managed to pant out at last.

'Nearly there!' the Queen repeated. 'Why, we passed it ten minutes ago! Faster!' And they ran on for a time in silence, with the wind whistling in Alice's ears, and almost blowing her hair off her head, she fancied.

'Now! Now!' cried the Queen. 'Faster! Faster!' And they went so fast that at last they seemed to skim through the air, hardly touching the ground with their feet, till suddenly, just as Alice was getting quite exhausted, they stopped, and she found herself sitting on the ground, breathless and giddy.

The Queen propped her up against a tree, and said kindly, 'You may rest a little now.'

Alice looked round her in great surprise. 'Why, I do believe we've been under this tree the whole time! Everything's just as it was!'

'Of course it is,' said the Queen, 'what would you have it?'

'Well, in *our* country,' said Alice, still panting a little, 'you'd generally get to somewhere else—if you ran very fast for a long time, as we've been doing.'

'A slow sort of country!' said the Queen. 'Now, *here*, you see, it takes all the running *you* can do, to keep in the same place. If you want to get somewhere else, you must run at least twice as fast as that!'

'I'd rather not try, please!' said Alice. 'I'm quite content to stay here—only I *am* so hot and thirsty!'

'I know what *you'd* like!' the Queen said good-naturedly, taking a little box out of her pocket. 'Have a biscuit?'

Alice thought it would not be civil to say 'No,' though it wasn't at all what she wanted. So she took it, and ate it

as well as she could: and it was *very* dry; and she thought she had never been so nearly choked in all her life.

'While you're refreshing yourself,' said the Queen, 'I'll just take the measurements.' And she took a ribbon out of her pocket, marked in inches, and began measuring the ground, and sticking little pegs in here and there.

'At the end of two yards,' she said, putting in a peg to mark the distance, 'I shall give you your directions—have another biscuit?'

'No, thank you,' said Alice: 'one's *quite* enough!'

'Thirst quenched, I hope?' said the Queen.

Alice did not know what to say to this, but luckily the Queen did not wait for an answer, but went on. 'At the end of *three* yards I shall repeat them—for fear of your forgetting them. At the end of *four*, I shall say good-bye. And at the end of *five*, I shall go!'

She had got all the pegs put in by this time, and Alice looked on with great interest as she returned to the tree, and then began slowly walking down the row.

At the two-yard peg she faced round, and said, 'A pawn goes two squares in its first move, you know. So you'll go *very* quickly through the Third Square—by railway, I should think—and you'll find yourself in the Fourth Square in no time. Well, *that* square belongs to Tweedledum and Tweedledee—the Fifth is mostly water—the Sixth belongs to Humpty Dumpty—But you make no remark?'

'I—I didn't know I had to make one—just then,' Alice faltered out.

'You *should* have said, "It's extremely kind of you to tell me all this"—however, we'll suppose it said—the Seventh Square is all forest—however, one of the Knights will show you the way—and in the Eighth Square we shall be Queens together, and it's all feasting and fun!' Alice got up and curtseyed, and sat down again.

At the next peg the Queen turned again, and this time she said, 'Speak in French when you can't think of the English for a thing—turn out your toes as you walk—and remember who you are!' She did not wait for Alice to curtsey this time, but walked on quickly to the next peg, where she turned for a moment to say 'good-bye,' and then hurried on to the last.

How it happened, Alice never knew, but exactly as she came to the last peg, she was gone. Whether she vanished into the air, or whether she ran quickly into the wood ('and she *can* run very fast!' thought Alice), there was no way of guessing, but she was gone, and Alice began to remember that she was a Pawn, and that it would soon be time for her to move.

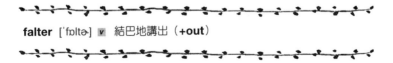

falter ['fɔltə] **v** 結巴地講出（**+out**）

03 ⁄

Looking-Glass Insects

Of course the first thing to do was to make a grand survey of the country she was going to travel through. 'It's something very like learning geography,' thought Alice, as she stood on tiptoe in hopes of being able to see a little further. 'Principal rivers—there *are* none. Principal mountains—I'm on the only one, but I don't think it's got any name. Principal towns—why, what *are* those creatures, making honey down there? They can't be bees—nobody ever saw bees a mile off, you know—' and for some time she stood silent, watching one of them that was bustling about among the flowers, poking its proboscis into them, 'just as if it was a regular bee,' thought Alice.

However, this was anything but a regular bee: in fact it was an elephant—as Alice soon found out, though the

proboscis [prə'bɑsɪs] *n* 能吸吮、取食、覺觸的管狀器官

idea quite took her breath away at first. 'And what enormous flowers they must be!' was her next idea. 'Something like cottages with the roofs taken off, and stalks put to them—and what quantities of honey they must make! I think I'll go down and—no, I won't*just* yet,' she went on, checking herself just as she was beginning to run down the hill, and trying to find some excuse for turning shy so suddenly. 'It'll never do to go down among them without a good long branch to brush them away— and what fun it'll be when they ask me how I like my walk. I shall say—"Oh, I like it well enough—"' (here came the favourite little toss of the head), '"only it was so dusty and hot, and the elephants did tease so!"'

'I think I'll go down the other way,' she said after a pause: 'and perhaps I may visit the elephants later on. Besides, I do so want to get into the Third Square!'

So with this excuse she ran down the hill and jumped over the first of the six little brooks.

'Tickets, please!' said the Guard, putting his head in at the window. In a moment everybody was holding out a ticket: they were about the same size as the people, and quite seemed to fill the carriage.

'Now then! Show your ticket, child!' the Guard went

on, looking angrily at Alice. And a great many voices all said together ('like the chorus of a song,' thought Alice), 'Don't keep him waiting, child! Why, his time is worth a thousand pounds a minute!'

'I'm afraid I haven't got one,' Alice said in a frightened tone: 'there wasn't a ticket-office where I came from.' And again the chorus of voices went on. 'There wasn't room for one where she came from. The land there is worth a thousand pounds an inch!'

'Don't make excuses,' said the Guard: 'you should have bought one from the engine-driver.' And once more the chorus of voices went on with 'The man that drives the engine. Why, the smoke alone is worth a thousand pounds a puff!'

Alice thought to herself, 'Then there's no use in speaking.' The voices didn't join in this time, as she hadn't spoken, but to her great surprise, they all *thought* in chorus (I hope you understand what *thinking in chorus* means— for I must confess that *I* don't), 'Better say nothing at all. Language is worth a thousand pounds a word!'

'I shall dream about a thousand pounds tonight, I know I shall!' thought Alice.

All this time the Guard was looking at her, first through a telescope, then through a microscope, and then through an opera-glass. At last he said, 'You're travelling the wrong way,' and shut up the window and went away.

'So young a child,' said the gentleman sitting opposite
to her (he was dressed in white paper), 'ought to know
which way she's going, even if she doesn't know her own
name!'

A Goat, that was sitting next to the gentleman in
white, shut his eyes and said in a loud voice, 'She ought to
know her way to the ticket-office, even if she doesn't
know her alphabet!'

There was a Beetle sitting next to the Goat (it was a
very queer carriage-full of passengers altogether), and, as
the rule seemed to be that they should all speak in turn, *he*
went on with 'She'll have to go back from here as luggage!'

Alice couldn't see who was sitting beyond the Beetle,

but a hoarse voice spoke next. 'Change engines—' it said, and was obliged to leave off.

'It sounds like a horse,' Alice thought to herself. And an extremely small voice, close to her ear, said, 'You might make a joke on that—something about "horse" and "hoarse," you know.'

Then a very gentle voice in the distance said, 'She must be labelled "Lass, with care," you know—'

And after that other voices went on ('What a number of people there are in the carriage!' thought Alice), saying, 'She must go by post, as she's got a head on her—' 'She must be sent as a message by the telegraph—' 'She must draw the train herself the rest of the way—' and so on.

But the gentleman dressed in white paper leaned forwards and whispered in her ear, 'Never mind what they all say, my dear, but take a return-ticket every time the train stops.'

'Indeed I shan't!' Alice said rather impatiently. 'I don't belong to this railway journey at all—I was in a wood just now—and I wish I could get back there.'

'You might make a joke on *that*,' said the little voice close to her ear: 'something about "you *would* if you could," you know.'

'Don't tease so,' said Alice, looking about in vain to see where the voice came from; 'if you're so anxious to have a joke made, why don't you make one yourself?'

The little voice sighed deeply: it was *very* unhappy, evidently, and Alice would have said something pitying to comfort it, 'If it would only sigh like other people!' she thought. But this was such a wonderfully small sigh, that she wouldn't have heard it at all, if it hadn't come *quite* close to her ear. The consequence of this was that it tickled her ear very much, and quite took off her thoughts from the unhappiness of the poor little creature.

'I know you are a friend,' the little voice went on; 'a dear friend, and an old friend. And you won't hurt me, though I *am* an insect.'

'What kind of insect?' Alice inquired a little anxiously. What she really wanted to know was, whether it could sting or not, but she thought this wouldn't be quite a civil question to ask.

'What, then you don't—' the little voice began, when it was drowned by a shrill scream from the engine, and everybody jumped up in alarm, Alice among the rest.

The Horse, who had put his head out of the window, quietly drew it in and said, 'It's only a brook we have to jump over.' Everybody seemed satisfied with this, though Alice felt a little nervous at the idea of trains jumping at

consequence [ˈkɑnsəˌkwɛns] *n* 結果，後果

all. 'However, it'll take us into the Fourth Square, that's some comfort!' she said to herself. In another moment she felt the carriage rise straight up into the air, and in her fright she caught at the thing nearest to her hand, which happened to be the Goat's beard.

But the beard seemed to melt away as she touched it, and she found herself sitting quietly under a tree—while the Gnat (for that was the insect she had been talking to) was balancing itself on a twig just over her head, and fanning her with its wings.

It certainly was a *very* large Gnat: 'about the size of a chicken,' Alice thought. Still, she couldn't feel nervous with it, after they had been talking together so long.

'—then you don't like all insects?' the Gnat went on, as quietly as if nothing had happened.

'I like them when they can talk,' Alice said. 'None of them ever talk, where *I* come from.'

'What sort of insects do you rejoice in, where *you* come from?' the Gnat inquired.

rejoice [rɪˈdʒɔɪs] **v** 喜歡；欣喜

'I don't *rejoice* in insects at all,' Alice explained, 'because I'm rather afraid of them—at least the large kinds. But I can tell you the names of some of them.'

'Of course they answer to their names?' the Gnat remarked carelessly.

'I never knew them to do it.'

'What's the use of their having names,' the Gnat said, 'if they won't answer to them?'

'No use to *them*,' said Alice; 'but it's useful to the people who name them, I suppose. If not, why do things have names at all?'

'I can't say,' the Gnat replied. 'Further on, in the wood down there, they've got no names—however, go on with your list of insects: you're wasting time.'

'Well, there's the Horse-fly,' Alice began, counting off the names on her fingers.

'All right,' said the Gnat: 'half way up that bush, you'll see a Rocking-horse-fly, if you look. It's made entirely of wood, and gets about by swinging itself from branch to branch.'

'What does it live on?' Alice asked, with great curiosity.

'Sap and sawdust,' said the Gnat. 'Go on with the list.'

Alice looked up at the Rocking-horse-fly with great interest, and made up her mind that it must have been just repainted, it looked so bright and sticky; and then she went on.

'And there's the Dragon-fly.'

'Look on the branch above your head,' said the Gnat, 'and there you'll find a snap-dragon-fly. Its body is made of plum-pudding, its wings of holly-leaves, and its head is a raisin burning in brandy.'

'And what does it live on?'

'Frumenty and mince pie,' the Gnat replied; 'and it makes its nest in a Christmas box.'

'And then there's the Butterfly,' Alice went on, after she had taken a good look at the insect with its head on fire, and had thought to herself, 'I wonder if that's the reason insects are so fond of flying into candles—because they want to turn into Snap-dragon-flies!'

'Crawling at your feet,' said the Gnat (Alice drew her

feet back in some alarm), 'you may observe a Bread-and-Butterfly. Its wings are thin slices of Bread-and-butter, its body is a crust,

and its head is a lump of sugar.'

'And what does *it* live on?'

'Weak tea with cream in it.'

A new difficulty came into Alice's head. 'Supposing it couldn't find any?' she suggested.

'Then it would die, of course.'

'But that must happen very often,' Alice remarked thoughtfully.

'It always happens,' said the Gnat.

After this, Alice was silent for a minute or two, pondering. The Gnat amused itself meanwhile by humming round and round her head: at last it settled again and remarked, 'I suppose you don't want to lose your name?'

'No, indeed,' Alice said, a little anxiously.

ponder ['pɑndə] **v** 仔細考慮;沉思

'And yet I don't know,' the Gnat went on in a careless tone: 'only think how convenient it would be if you could manage to go home without it! For instance, if the governess wanted to call you to your lessons, she would call out "come here——," and there she would have to leave off, because there wouldn't be any name for her to call, and of course you wouldn't have to go, you know.'

'That would never do, I'm sure,' said Alice: 'the governess would never think of excusing me lessons for that. If she couldn't remember my name, she'd call me "Miss!" as the servants do.'

'Well, if she said "Miss," and didn't say anything more,' the Gnat remarked, 'of course you'd miss your lessons. That's a joke. I wish *you* had made it.'

'Why do you wish *I* had made it?' Alice asked. 'It's a very bad one.'

But the Gnat only sighed deeply, while two large tears came rolling down its cheeks.

'You shouldn't make jokes,' Alice said, 'if it makes you so unhappy.'

Then came another of those melancholy little sighs, and this time the poor Gnat really seemed to have sighed

convenient [kən'vinjənt] *adj* 方便的；便利的

itself away, for, when Alice looked up, there was nothing whatever to be seen on the twig, and, as she was getting quite chilly with sitting still so long, she got up and walked on.

She very soon came to an open field, with a wood on the other side of it: it looked much darker than the last wood, and Alice felt a *little* timid about going into it. However, on second thoughts, she made up her mind to go on: 'for I certainly won't go *back*,' she thought to herself, and this was the only way to the Eighth Square.

'This must be the wood,' she said thoughtfully to herself, 'where things have no names. I wonder what'll become of *my* name when I go in? I shouldn't like to lose it at all—because they'd have to give me another, and it would be almost certain to be an ugly one. But then the fun would be trying to find the creature that had got my old name! That's just like the advertisements, you know, when people lose dogs—"answers to the name of 'Dash:' had on a brass collar"—just fancy calling everything you met "Alice," till one of them answered! Only they wouldn't answer at all, if they were wise.'

She was rambling on in this way when she reached the wood: it looked very cool and shady. 'Well, at any rate it's a great comfort,' she said as she stepped under the trees, 'after being so hot, to get into the—into *what?*' she went on, rather surprised at not being able to think of the word. 'I mean to get under the—under the—under *this*,

you know!' putting her hand on the trunk of the tree. 'What *does* it call itself, I wonder? I do believe it's got no name—why, to be sure it hasn't!'

She stood silent for a minute, thinking: then she suddenly began again. 'Then it really *has* happened, after all! And now, who am I? I *will* remember, if I can! I'm determined to do it!' But being determined didn't help much, and all she could say, after a great deal of puzzling, was, 'L, I *know* it begins with L!'

Just then a Fawn came wandering by: it looked at Alice with its large gentle eyes, but didn't seem at all frightened. 'Here then! Here then!' Alice said, as she held out her hand and tried to stroke it; but it only started back a little, and then stood looking at her again.

'What do you call yourself?' the Fawn said at last. Such a soft sweet voice it had!

'I wish I knew!' thought poor Alice. She answered, rather sadly, 'Nothing, just now.'

'Think again,' it said: 'that won't do.'

Alice thought, but nothing came of it. 'Please, would you tell me what *you* call yourself?' she said timidly. 'I think that might help a little.'

'I'll tell you, if you'll move a little further on,' the Fawn said. 'I can't remember here.'

So they walked on together though the wood, Alice with her arms clasped lovingly round the soft neck of the

Fawn, till they came out into another open field, and here
the Fawn gave a sudden bound into the air, and shook
itself free from Alice's arms. 'I'm a Fawn!' it cried out in a
voice of delight, 'and, dear me! you're a human child!' A
sudden look of alarm came into its beautiful brown eyes,
and in another moment it had darted away at full speed.

Alice stood looking after it, almost ready to cry with

vexation at having lost her dear little fellow-traveller so suddenly. 'However, I know my name now.' she said, 'that's *some* comfort. Alice—Alice—I won't forget it again. And now, which of these finger-posts ought I to follow, I wonder?'

It was not a very difficult question to answer, as there was only one road through the wood, and the two finger-posts both pointed along it. 'I'll settle it,' Alice said to herself, 'when the road divides and they point different ways.'

But this did not seem likely to happen. She went on and on, a long way, but wherever the road divided there were sure to be two finger-posts pointing the same way, one marked 'TO TWEEDLEDUM'S HOUSE' and the other 'TO THE HOUSE OF TWEEDLEDEE.'

'I do believe,' said Alice at last, 'that they live in the same house! I wonder I never thought of that before—But I can't stay there long. I'll just call and say "how d'you do?" and ask them the way out of the wood. If I could only get to the Eighth Square before it gets dark!' So she wandered on, talking to herself as she went, till, on turning a sharp corner, she came upon two fat little men, so suddenly that she could not help starting back, but in another moment she recovered herself, feeling sure that they must be.

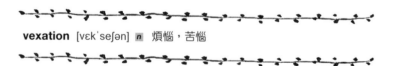

vexation [vɛkˈseʃən] *n* 煩惱，苦惱

Tweedledum and Tweedledee

They were standing under a tree, each with an arm round the other's neck, and Alice knew which was which in a moment, because one of them had 'DUM' embroidered on his collar, and the other 'DEE.' 'I suppose they've each got "TWEEDLE" round at the back of the collar,' she said to herself.

They stood so still that she quite forgot they were alive, and she was just looking round to see if the word "TWEEDLE" was written at the back of each collar, when she was startled by a voice coming from the one marked 'DUM.'

'If you think we're wax-works,' he said, 'you ought to pay, you know. Wax-works weren't made to be looked at for nothing, nohow!'

'Contrariwise,' added the one marked 'DEE,' 'if you think we're alive, you ought to speak.'

'I'm sure I'm very sorry,' was all Alice could say; for the words of the old song kept ringing through her head like the ticking of a clock, and she could hardly help saying them out loud:—

> *'Tweedledum and Tweedledee*
> *Agreed to have a battle;*
> *For Tweedledum said Tweedledee*
> *Had spoiled his nice new rattle.*
>
> *Just then flew down a monstrous crow,*
> *As black as a tar-barrel;*
> *Which frightened both the heroes so,*
> *They quite forgot their quarrel.'*

contrariwise [ˈkɑntrɛrɪˌwaɪz] *adv* 反之亦然

'I know what you're thinking about,' said Tweedledum: 'but it isn't so, nohow.'

'Contrariwise,' continued Tweedledee, 'if it was so, it might be; and if it were so, it would be; but as it isn't, it ain't. That's logic.'

'I was thinking,' Alice said very politely, 'which is the best way out of this wood: it's getting so dark. Would you tell me, please?'

But the little men only looked at each other and grinned.

They looked so exactly like a couple of great schoolboys, that Alice couldn't help pointing her finger at Tweedledum, and saying 'First Boy!'

'Nohow!' Tweedledum cried out briskly, and shut his mouth up again with a snap.

'Next Boy!' said Alice, passing on to Tweedledee, though she felt quite certain he would only shout out 'Contrariwise!' and so he did.

'You've been wrong!' cried Tweedledum. 'The first thing in a visit is to say "How d'ye do?" and shake hands!' And here the two brothers gave each other a hug, and then they held out the two hands that were free, to shake hands with her.

Alice did not like shaking hands with either of them first, for fear of hurting the other one's feelings; so, as the best way out of the difficulty, she took hold of both hands

at once: the next moment they were dancing round in a ring. This seemed quite natural (she remembered afterwards), and she was not even surprised to hear music playing: it seemed to come from the tree under which they were dancing, and it was done (as well as she could make it out) by the branches rubbing one across the other, like fiddles and fiddle-sticks.

'But it certainly *was* funny,' (Alice said afterwards, when she was telling her sister the history of all this,) 'to find myself singing "*Here we go round the mulberry bush.*" I don't know when I began it, but somehow I felt as if I'd been singing it a long long time!'

The other two dancers were fat, and very soon out of breath. 'Four times round is enough for one dance,' Tweedledum panted out, and they left off dancing as suddenly as they had begun: the music stopped at the same moment.

Then they let go of Alice's hands, and stood looking at her for a minute: there was a rather awkward pause, as Alice didn't know how to begin a conversation with people she had just been dancing with. 'It would never do to say "How d'ye do?" *now*,' she said to herself: 'we seem to have got beyond that, somehow!'

'I hope you're not much tired?' she said at last.

'Nohow. And thank you *very* much for asking,' said Tweedledum.

'So *much* obliged!' added Tweedledee. 'You like poetry?'

'Ye-es, pretty well—*some* poetry,' Alice said doubtfully. 'Would you tell me which road leads out of the wood?'

'What shall I repeat to her?' said Tweedledee, looking round at Tweedledum with great solemn eyes, and not noticing Alice's question.

'"*The Walrus and the Carpenter*" is the longest,' Tweedledum replied, giving his brother an affectionate hug.

Tweedledee began instantly:

'The sun was shining—'

Here Alice ventured to interrupt him. 'If it's *very* long,' she said, as politely as she could, 'would you please tell me first which road—'

Tweedledee smiled gently, and began again:

'The sun was shining on the sea,
Shining with all his might:
He did his very best to make
The billows smooth and bright—
And this was odd, because it was
The middle of the night.

The moon was shining sulkily,
Because she thought the sun
Had got no business to be there
After the day was done—
"It's very rude of him," she said,
"To come and spoil the fun!"

The sea was wet as wet could be,
The sands were dry as dry.
You could not see a cloud, because
No cloud was in the sky:
No birds were flying over head—
There were no birds to fly.

The Walrus and the Carpenter
Were walking close at hand;
They wept like anything to see
Such quantities of sand:
"If this were only cleared away,"
They said, "it would be grand!"

"If seven maids with seven mops
Swept it for half a year,
Do you suppose," the Walrus said,
"That they could get it clear?"
"I doubt it," said the Carpenter,
And shed a bitter tear.

"O Oysters, come and walk with us!"
The Walrus did beseech.
"A pleasant walk, a pleasant talk,
Along the briny beach:
We cannot do with more than four,
To give a hand to each."

The eldest Oyster looked at him.
But never a word he said:
The eldest Oyster winked his eye,
And shook his heavy head—
Meaning to say he did not choose
To leave the oyster-bed.

beseech [bɪˈsitʃ] **v** 懇求；哀求

But four young oysters hurried up,
All eager for the treat:
Their coats were brushed, their faces washed,
Their shoes were clean and neat—
And this was odd, because, you know,
They hadn't any feet.

Four other Oysters followed them,
And yet another four;
And thick and fast they came at last,
And more, and more, and more—
All hopping through the frothy waves,
And scrambling to the shore.

The Walrus and the Carpenter
Walked on a mile or so,
And then they rested on a rock
Conveniently low:
And all the little Oysters stood
And waited in a row.

"The time has come," the Walrus said,
"To talk of many things:
Of shoes—and ships—and sealing-wax—
Of cabbages—and kings—
And why the sea is boiling hot—
And whether pigs have wings."

"But wait a bit," the Oysters cried,
"Before we have our chat;
For some of us are out of breath,
And all of us are fat!"
"No hurry!" said the Carpenter.
They thanked him much for that.

"A loaf of bread," the Walrus said,
"Is what we chiefly need:
Pepper and vinegar besides
Are very good indeed—
Now if you're ready Oysters dear,

We can begin to feed."

"But not on us!" the Oysters cried,
Turning a little blue,
"After such kindness, that would be
A dismal thing to do!"
"The night is fine," the Walrus said
"Do you admire the view?

"It was so kind of you to come!
And you are very nice!"
The Carpenter said nothing but
"Cut us another slice:
I wish you were not quite so deaf—
I've had to ask you twice!"

"It seems a shame," the Walrus said,
"To play them such a trick,
After we've brought them out so far,
And made them trot so quick!"
The Carpenter said nothing but
"The butter's spread too thick!"

dismal [ˈdɪzml] *adj* 令人悲傷的；使人驚恐的

"I weep for you," the Walrus said.
"I deeply sympathize."
With sobs and tears he sorted out
Those of the largest size.
Holding his pocket handkerchief
Before his streaming eyes.

"O Oysters," said the Carpenter.
"You've had a pleasant run!
Shall we be trotting home again?"
But answer came there none—
And that was scarcely odd, because
They'd eaten every one.'

'I like the Walrus best,' said Alice: 'because you see he was a *little* sorry for the poor oysters.'

'He ate more than the Carpenter, though,' said Tweedledee. 'You see he held his handkerchief in front, so that the Carpenter couldn't count how many he took: contrariwise.'

'That was mean!' Alice said indignantly. 'Then I like the Carpenter best—if he didn't eat so many as the Walrus.'

'But he ate as many as he could get,' said Tweedledum.

This was a puzzler. After a pause, Alice began, 'Well! They were *both* very unpleasant characters—' Here she checked herself in some alarm, at hearing something that sounded to her like the puffing of a large steam-engine in the wood near them, though she feared it was more likely to be a wild beast. 'Are there any lions or tigers about here?' she asked timidly.

'It's only the Red King snoring,' said Tweedledee.

'Come and look at him!' the brothers cried, and they each took one of Alice's hands, and led her up to where the King was sleeping.

'Isn't he a *lovely* sight?' said Tweedledum.

Alice couldn't say honestly that he was. He had a tall

indignantly [ɪnˈdɪgnəntlɪ] **adv** 憤慨地，憤憤不平地

red night-cap
on, with a
tassel, and he
was lying
crumpled up
into a sort of
untidy heap,
and snoring
loud—'fit to

snore his head off!' as Tweedledum remarked.

'I'm afraid he'll catch cold with lying on the damp grass,' said Alice, who was a very thoughtful little girl.

'He's dreaming now,' said Tweedledee: 'and what do you think he's dreaming about?'

Alice said 'Nobody can guess that.'

'Why, about *you!*' Tweedledee exclaimed, clapping his hands triumphantly. 'And if he left off dreaming about you, where do you suppose you'd be?'

'Where I am now, of course,' said Alice.

'Not you!' Tweedledee retorted contemptuously. 'You'd be nowhere. Why, you're only a sort of thing in his dream!'

'If that there King was to wake,' added Tweedledum, 'you'd go out—bang!—just like a candle!'

'I shouldn't!' Alice exclaimed indignantly. 'Besides, if *I'm* only a sort of thing in his dream, what are *you*, I should like to know?'

'Ditto' said Tweedledum.

'Ditto, ditto' cried Tweedledee.

He shouted this so loud that Alice couldn't help saying, 'Hush! You'll be waking him, I'm afraid, if you make so much noise.'

'Well, it no use *your* talking about waking him,' said Tweedledum, 'when you're only one of the things in his dream. You know very well you're not real.'

'I *am* real!' said Alice and began to cry.

'You won't make yourself a bit realler by crying,' Tweedledee remarked: 'there's nothing to cry about.'

'If I wasn't real,' Alice said—half-laughing through her tears, it all seemed so ridiculous—'I shouldn't be able to cry.'

'I hope you don't suppose those are real tears?' Tweedledum interrupted in a tone of great contempt.

'I know they're talking nonsense,' Alice thought to herself: 'and it's foolish to cry about it.' So she brushed away her tears, and went on as cheerfully as she could. 'At any rate I'd better be getting out of the wood, for really it's coming on very dark. Do you think it's going to rain?'

Tweedledum spread a large umbrella over himself and his brother, and looked up into it. 'No, I don't think it is,' he said: 'at least—not under *here*. Nohow.'

'But it may rain *outside*?'

'It may—if it chooses,' said Tweedledee: 'we've no objection. Contrariwise.'

'Selfish things!' thought Alice, and she was just going to say 'Good-night' and leave them, when Tweedledum sprang out from under the umbrella and seized her by the wrist.

'Do you see *that*?' he said, in a voice choking with passion, and his eyes grew large and yellow all in a moment, as he pointed with a trembling finger at a small white thing lying under the tree.

'It's only a rattle,' Alice said, after a careful examination of the little white thing. 'Not a rattle-snake, you know,' she added hastily, thinking that he was frightened: 'only an old rattle—quite old and broken.'

'I knew it was!' cried Tweedledum, beginning to stamp about wildly and tear his hair. 'It's spoilt, of course!' Here

he looked at Tweedledee, who immediately sat down on the ground, and tried to hide himself under the umbrella.

Alice laid her hand upon his arm, and said in a soothing tone, 'You needn't be so angry about an old rattle.'

'But it isn't old!' Tweedledum cried, in a greater fury than ever. 'It's new, I tell you—I bought it yesterday—my nice new RATTLE!' and his voice rose to a perfect scream.

All this time Tweedledee was trying his best to fold up the umbrella, with himself in it: which was such an extraordinary thing to do, that it quite took off Alice's attention from the angry brother. But he couldn't quite succeed, and it ended in his rolling over, bundled up in the umbrella, with only his head out: and there he lay, opening and shutting his mouth and his large eyes—'looking more like a fish than anything else,' Alice thought.

'Of course you agree to have a battle?' Tweedledum said in a calmer tone.

'I suppose so,' the other sulkily replied, as he crawled out of the umbrella: 'only *she* must help us to dress up, you know.'

So the two brothers went off hand-in-hand into the wood, and returned in a minute with their arms full of things—such as bolsters, blankets, hearth-rugs, table-cloths, dish-covers and coal-scuttles. 'I hope you're a good hand at pinning and tying strings?' Tweedledum remarked. 'Every one of these things has got to go on, somehow or other.'

Alice said afterwards she had never seen such a fuss made about anything in all her life—the way those two bustled about—and the quantity of things they put on—and the trouble they gave her in tying strings and fastening buttons—'Really they'll be more like bundles of old clothes than anything else, by the time they're ready!' she said to herself, as she arranged a bolster round the neck of Tweedledee, 'to keep his head from being cut off,' as he said.

'You know,' he added very gravely, 'it's one of the

gravely ['grevlɪ] *adv* 嚴肅地，莊重地

most serious things that can possibly happen to one in a battle—to get one's head cut off.'

Alice laughed aloud: but she managed to turn it into a cough, for fear of hurting his feelings.

'Do I look very pale?' said Tweedledum, coming up to have his helmet tied on. (He *called* it a helmet, though it certainly looked much more like a saucepan.)

'Well—yes—a *little*,' Alice replied gently.

'I'm very brave generally,' he went on in a low voice: 'only to-day I happen to have a headache.'

'And *I've* got a toothache!' said Tweedledee, who had overheard the remark. 'I'm far worse off than you!'

'Then you'd better not fight to-day,' said Alice, thinking it a good opportunity to make peace.

'We *must* have a bit of a fight, but I don't care about going on long,' said Tweedledum. 'What's the time now?'

Tweedledee looked at his watch, and said 'Half-past four.'

'Let's fight till six, and then have dinner,' said Tweedledum.

'Very well,' the other said, rather sadly: 'and *she* can watch us—only you'd better not come *very* close,' he added: 'I generally hit everything I can see—when I get really excited.'

'And *I* hit everything within reach,' cried Tweedledum, 'whether I can see it or not!'

Alice laughed. 'You must hit the *trees* pretty often, I should think,' she said.

Tweedledum looked round him with a satisfied smile. 'I don't suppose,' he said, 'there'll be a tree left standing, for ever so far round, by the time we've finished!'

'And all about a rattle!' said Alice, still hoping to make them a *little* ashamed of fighting for such a trifle.

'I shouldn't have minded it so much,' said Tweedledum, 'if it hadn't been a new one.'

'I wish the monstrous crow would come!' thought Alice.

'There's only one sword, you know,' Tweedledum said to his brother: 'but you can have the umbrella—it's quite as sharp. Only we must begin quick. It's getting as dark as it can.'

'And darker,' said Tweedledee.

It was getting dark so suddenly that Alice thought there must be a thunderstorm coming on. 'What a thick black cloud that is!' she said. 'And how fast it comes! Why, I do believe it's got wings!'

'It's the crow!' Tweedledum cried out in a shrill voice of alarm: and the two brothers took to their heels and

trifle ['traɪfl] *n* 小事，瑣事

were out of sight in a moment.

Alice ran a little way into the wood, and stopped under a large tree. 'It can never get at me *here*,' she thought: 'it's far too large to squeeze itself in among the trees. But I wish it wouldn't flap its wings so—it makes quite a hurricane in the wood—here's somebody's shawl being blown away!'

05 ╱

Wool and Water

She caught the shawl as she spoke, and looked about for the owner: in another moment the White Queen came running wildly through the wood, with both arms stretched out wide, as if she were flying, and Alice very civilly went to meet her with the shawl.

'I'm very glad I happened to be in the way,' Alice said, as she helped her to put on her shawl again.

The White Queen only looked at her in a helpless frightened sort of way, and kept repeating something in a whisper to herself that sounded like 'bread-and-butter, bread-and-butter,' and Alice felt that if there was to be any conversation at all, she must manage it herself. So she began rather timidly: 'Am I addressing the White Queen?'

'Well, yes, if you call that a-dressing,' The Queen said.

address [ə'drɛs] **v** 交談；穿衣（作者在此以這兩個語意玩起文字遊戲）

'It isn't *my* notion of the thing, at all.'

Alice thought it would never do to have an argument at the very beginning of their conversation, so she smiled and said, 'If your Majesty will only tell me the right way to begin, I'll do it as well as I can.'

'But I don't want it done at all!' groaned the poor Queen. 'I've been a-dressing myself for the last two hours.'

It would have been all the better, as it seemed to Alice, if she had got some one else to dress her, she was so dreadfully untidy. 'Every single thing's crooked,' Alice thought to herself, 'and she's all over pins!—may I put your shawl straight for you?' she added aloud.

'I don't know what's the matter with it!' the Queen said, in a melancholy voice. 'It's out of temper, I think. I've pinned it here, and I've pinned it there, but there's no pleasing it!'

'It *can't* go straight, you know, if you pin it all on one side,' Alice said, as she gently put it right for her; 'and, dear me, what a state your hair is in!'

'The brush has got entangled in it!' the Queen said with a sigh. 'And I lost the comb yesterday.'

Alice carefully released the brush, and did her best to

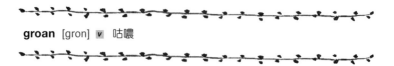

groan [gron] **v** 咕噥

get the hair into order. 'Come, you look rather better now!' she said, after altering most of the pins. 'But really you should have a lady's maid!'

'I'm sure I'll take you with pleasure!' the Queen said. 'Twopence a week, and jam every other day.'

Alice couldn't help laughing, as she said, 'I don't want you to hire *me*—and I don't care for jam.'

'It's very good jam,' said the Queen.

'Well, I don't want any *to-day*, at any rate.'

'You couldn't have it if you *did* want it,' the Queen said. 'The rule is, jam to-morrow and jam yesterday—but never jam to-day.'

'It *must* come sometimes to "jam to-day,"' Alice objected.

'No, it can't,' said the Queen. 'It's jam every *other* day: to-day isn't any *other* day, you know.'

'I don't understand you,' said Alice. 'It's dreadfully confusing!'

'That's the effect of living backwards,' the Queen said kindly: 'it always makes one a little giddy at first—'

'Living backwards!' Alice repeated in great astonishment. 'I never heard of such a thing!'

'—but there's one great advantage in it, that one's memory works both ways.'

'I'm sure *mine* only works one way,' Alice remarked. 'I can't remember things before they happen.'

'It's a poor sort of memory that only works backwards,' the Queen remarked.

'What sort of things do *you* remember best?' Alice ventured to ask.

'Oh, things that happened the week after next,' the Queen replied in a careless tone. 'For instance, now,' she went on, sticking a large piece of plaster [band-aid] on her finger as she spoke, 'there's the King's Messenger. He's in

prison now, being punished: and the trial doesn't even begin till next Wednesday: and of course the crime comes last of all.'

'Suppose he never commits the crime?' said Alice.

'That would be all the better, wouldn't it?' the Queen said, as she bound the plaster round her finger with a bit of ribbon.

Alice felt there was no denying *that*. 'Of course it would be all the better,' she said: 'but it wouldn't be all the better his being punished.'

'You're wrong *there*, at any rate,' said the Queen: 'were *you* ever punished?'

'Only for faults,' said Alice.

'And you were all the better for it, I know!' the Queen said triumphantly.

'Yes, but then I *had* done the things I was punished for,' said Alice: 'that makes all the difference.'

'But if you *hadn't* done them,' the Queen said, 'that would have been better still; better, and better, and better!' Her voice went higher with each 'better,' till it got quite to a squeak at last.

Alice was just beginning to say 'There's a mistake somewhere—,' when the Queen began screaming so loud that she had to leave the sentence unfinished. 'Oh, oh, oh!' shouted the Queen, shaking her hand about as if she wanted to shake it off. 'My finger's bleeding! Oh, oh, oh, oh!'

Her screams were so exactly like the whistle of a steam-engine, that Alice had to hold both her hands over her ears.

'What *is* the matter?' she said, as soon as there was a chance of making herself heard. 'Have you pricked your finger?'

'I haven't pricked it *yet*,' the Queen said, 'but I soon shall—oh, oh, oh!'

'When do you expect to do it?' Alice asked, feeling very much inclined to laugh.

'When I fasten my shawl again,' the poor Queen groaned out: 'the brooch will come undone directly. Oh, oh!' As she said the words the brooch flew open, and the Queen clutched wildly at it, and tried to clasp it again.

'Take care!' cried Alice. 'You're holding it all crooked!' And she caught at the brooch; but it was too late: the pin had slipped, and the Queen had pricked her finger.

'That accounts for the bleeding, you see,' she said to Alice with a smile. 'Now you understand the way things happen here.'

'But why don't you scream now?' Alice asked, holding

inclined [ɪnˈklaɪnd] *adj* 傾向於

brooch [brotʃ] *n* 女用胸針（或領針）

her hands ready to put over her ears again.

'Why, I've done all the screaming already,' said the Queen. 'What would be the good of having it all over again?'

By this time it was getting light. 'The crow must have flown away, I think,' said Alice: 'I'm so glad it's gone. I thought it was the night coming on.'

'I wish *I* could manage to be glad!' the Queen said. 'Only I never can remember the rule. You must be very happy, living in this wood, and being glad whenever you like!'

'Only it is so *very* lonely here!' Alice said in a melancholy voice; and at the thought of her loneliness two large tears came rolling down her cheeks.

'Oh, don't go on like that!' cried the poor Queen, wringing her hands in despair. 'Consider what a great girl you are. Consider what a long way you've come to-day. Consider what o'clock it is. Consider anything, only don't cry!'

Alice could not help laughing at this, even in the midst of her tears. 'Can *you* keep from crying by considering things?' she asked.

'That's the way it's done,' the Queen said with great decision: 'nobody can do two things at once, you know. Let's consider your age to begin with—how old are you?'

'I'm seven and a half exactly.'

'You needn't say "exactually,"' the Queen remarked: 'I

can believe it without that. Now I'll give *you* something to believe. I'm just one hundred and one, five months and a day.'

'I can't believe *that*!' said Alice.

'Can't you?' the Queen said in a pitying tone. 'Try again: draw a long breath, and shut your eyes.'

Alice laughed. 'There's no use trying,' she said: 'one *can't* believe impossible things.'

'I daresay you haven't had much practice,' said the Queen. 'When I was your age, I always did it for half-an-hour a day. Why, sometimes I've believed as many as six impossible things before breakfast. There goes the shawl again!'

The brooch had come undone as she spoke, and a sudden gust of wind blew the Queen's shawl across a little brook. The Queen spread out her arms again, and went flying after it, and this time she succeeded in catching it for herself. 'I've got it!' she cried in a triumphant tone. 'Now you shall see me pin it on again, all by myself!'

'Then I hope your finger is better now?' Alice said very politely, as she crossed the little brook after the Queen.

♠ ♥ ♣ ♦

triumphant [traɪˈʌmfənt] *adj* 得意洋洋的

'Oh, much better!' cried the Queen, her voice rising to a squeak as she went on. 'Much be-etter! Be-etter! Be-e-e-etter! Be-e-ehh!' The last word ended in a long bleat, so like a sheep that Alice quite started.

She looked at the Queen, who seemed to have suddenly wrapped herself up in wool. Alice rubbed her eyes, and looked again. She couldn't make out what had happened at all. Was she in a shop? And was that really— was it really a *sheep* that was sitting on the other side of the counter? Rub as she could, she could make nothing more of it: she was in a little dark shop, leaning with her elbows on the counter, and opposite to her was an old Sheep, sitting in an arm-chair knitting, and every now and then leaving off to look at her through a great pair of spectacles.

'What is it you want to buy?' the Sheep said at last, looking up for a moment from her knitting.

'I don't *quite* know yet,' Alice said, very gently. 'I should like to look all round me first, if I might.'

'You may look in front of you, and on both sides, if you like,' said the Sheep: 'but you can't look *all* round you—unless you've got eyes at the back of your head.'

But these, as it happened, Alice had *not* got: so she contented herself with turning round, looking at the shelves as she came to them.

The shop seemed to be full of all manner of curious

things—but the oddest part of it all was, that whenever she looked hard at any shelf, to make out exactly what it had on it, that particular shelf was always quite empty: though the others round it were crowded as full as they could hold.

'Things flow about so here!' she said at last in a

plaintive tone, after she had spent a minute or so in vainly pursuing a large bright thing, that looked sometimes like a doll and sometimes like a work-box, and was always in the shelf next above the one she was looking at. 'And this one is the most provoking of all—but I'll tell you what—' she added, as a sudden thought struck her, 'I'll follow it up to the very top shelf of all. It'll puzzle it to go through the ceiling, I expect!'

But even this plan failed: the 'thing' went through the ceiling as quietly as possible, as if it were quite used to it.

'Are you a child or a teetotum?' the Sheep said, as she took up another pair of needles. 'You'll make me giddy soon, if you go on turning round like that.' She was now working with fourteen pairs at once, and Alice couldn't help looking at her in great astonishment.

'How *can* she knit with so many?' the puzzled child thought to herself. 'She gets more and more like a porcupine every minute!'

'Can you row?' the Sheep asked, handing her a pair of knitting-needles as she spoke.

'Yes, a little—but not on land—and not with needles—' Alice was beginning to say, when suddenly the

plaintive ['plentɪv] *adj* 悲傷的，憂鬱的，哀愁的

needles turned into oars in her hands, and she found they were in a little boat, gliding along between banks: so there was nothing for it but to do her best.

'Feather!' cried the Sheep, as she took up another pair

feather [ˈfɛðə] *v* 平槳 *n* 羽毛（作者在此以這兩個語意玩起文字遊戲）

of needles.

This didn't sound like a remark that needed any answer, so Alice said nothing, but pulled away. There was something very queer about the water, she thought, as every now and then the oars got fast in it, and would hardly come out again.

'Feather! Feather!' the Sheep cried again, taking more needles. 'You'll be catching a crab directly.'

'A dear little crab!' thought Alice. 'I should like that.'

'Didn't you hear me say "Feather"?' the Sheep cried angrily, taking up quite a bunch of needles.

'Indeed I did,' said Alice: 'you've said it very often—and very loud. Please, where *are* the crabs?'

'In the water, of course!' said the Sheep, sticking some of the needles into her hair, as her hands were full. 'Feather, I say!'

'*Why* do you say "feather" so often?' Alice asked at last, rather vexed. 'I'm not a bird!'

'You are,' said the Sheep: 'you're a little goose.'

This offended Alice a little, so there was no more conversation for a minute or two, while the boat glided gently on, sometimes among beds of weeds (which made

catch a crab [kætʃ] [ə] [kræb] 划船時用槳不當，導致船槳拔不出來：抓螃蟹（作者在此以這兩個語意玩起文字遊戲）

the oars stick fast in the water, worse then ever), and sometimes under trees, but always with the same tall river-banks frowning over their heads.

'Oh, please! There are some scented rushes!' Alice cried in a sudden transport of delight. 'There really are—and *such* beauties!'

'You needn't say "please" to *me* about 'em,' the Sheep said, without looking up from her knitting: 'I didn't put 'em there, and I'm not going to take 'em away.'

'No, but I meant—please, may we wait and pick some?' Alice pleaded. 'If you don't mind stopping the boat for a minute.'

'How am *I* to stop it?' said the Sheep. 'If you leave off rowing, it'll stop of itself.'

So the boat was left to drift down the stream as it would, till it glided gently in among the waving rushes. And then the little sleeves were carefully rolled up, and the little arms were plunged in elbow-deep to get the rushes a good long way down before breaking them off—and for a while Alice forgot all about the Sheep and the knitting, as she bent over the side of the boat, with just the ends of her tangled hair dipping into the water—while with bright eager eyes she caught at one bunch after another of the darling scented rushes.

'I only hope the boat won't tipple over!' she said to herself. 'Oh, *what* a lovely one! Only I couldn't quite reach

it.' 'And it certainly *did* seem a little provoking ('almost as if it happened on purpose,' she thought) that, though she managed to pick plenty of beautiful rushes as the boat glided by, there was always a more lovely one that she couldn't reach.

'The prettiest are always further!' she said at last, with a sigh at the obstinacy of the rushes in growing so far off, as, with flushed cheeks and dripping hair and hands, she scrambled back into her place, and began to arrange her new-found treasures.

What mattered it to her just then that the rushes had begun to fade, and to lose all their scent and beauty, from the very moment that she picked them? Even real scented rushes, you know, last only a very little while—and these, being dream-rushes, melted away almost like snow, as they lay in heaps at her feet—but Alice hardly noticed this, there were so many other curious things to think about.

They hadn't gone much farther before the blade of one of the oars got fast in the water and *wouldn't* come out again (so Alice explained it afterwards), and the consequence was that the handle of it caught her under the chin, and, in spite of a series of little shrieks of 'Oh,

obstinacy [ˈɑbstənəsɪ] *n* 頑固；（病痛等的）難治

oh, oh!' from poor Alice, it swept her straight off the seat, and down among the heap of rushes.

However, she wasn't hurt, and was soon up again: the Sheep went on with her knitting all the while, just as if nothing had happened. 'That was a nice crab you caught!' she remarked, as Alice got back into her place, very much relieved to find herself still in the boat.

'Was it? I didn't see it,' Said Alice, peeping cautiously over the side of the boat into the dark water. 'I wish it hadn't let go—I should so like to see a little crab to take home with me!' But the Sheep only laughed scornfully, and went on with her knitting.

'Are there many crabs here?' said Alice.

'Crabs, and all sorts of things,' said the Sheep: 'plenty of choice, only make up your mind. Now, what *do* you want to buy?'

'To buy!' Alice echoed in a tone that was half astonished and half frightened—for the oars, and the boat, and the river, had vanished all in a moment, and she was back again in the little dark shop.

'I should like to buy an egg, please,' she said timidly. 'How do you sell them?'

'Fivepence farthing for one—Twopence for two,' the Sheep replied.

'Then two are cheaper than one?' Alice said in a surprised tone, taking out her purse.

'Only you *must* eat them both, if you buy two,' said the Sheep.

'Then I'll have *one*, please,' said Alice, as she put the money down on the counter. For she thought to herself, 'They mightn't be at all nice, you know.'

The Sheep took the money, and put it away in a box: then she said 'I never put things into people's hands—that would never do—you must get it for yourself.' And so saying, she went off to the other end of the shop, and set the egg upright on a shelf.

'I wonder *why* it wouldn't do?' thought Alice, as she groped her way among the tables and chairs, for the shop was very dark towards the end. 'The egg seems to get further away the more I walk towards it. Let me see, is this a chair? Why, it's got branches, I declare! How very odd to find trees growing here! And actually here's a little brook! Well, this is the very queerest shop I ever saw!'

So she went on, wondering more and more at every step, as everything turned into a tree the moment she came up to it, and she quite expected the egg to do the same.

06 /

Humpty Dumpty

However, the egg only got larger and larger, and more and more human: when she had come within a few yards of it, she saw that it had eyes and a nose and mouth; and when she had come close to it, she saw clearly that it was HUMPTY DUMPTY himself. 'It can't be anybody else!' she said to herself. 'I'm as certain of it, as if his name were written all over his face.'

It might have been written a hundred times, easily, on that enormous face. Humpty Dumpty was sitting with his legs crossed, like a Turk, on the top of a high wall—such a narrow one that Alice quite wondered how he could keep his balance—and, as his eyes were steadily fixed in the opposite direction, and he didn't take the least notice of her, she thought he must be a stuffed figure after all.

'And how exactly like an egg he is!' she said aloud, standing with her hands ready to catch him, for she was every moment expecting him to fall.

'It's *very* provoking,' Humpty Dumpty said after a

long silence, looking away from Alice as he spoke, 'to be called an egg—Very!'

'I said you *looked* like an egg, Sir,' Alice gently explained. 'And some eggs are very pretty, you know' she added, hoping to turn her remark into a sort of a compliment.

'Some people,' said Humpty Dumpty, looking away from her as usual, 'have no more sense than a baby!'

Alice didn't know what to say to this: it wasn't at all like conversation, she thought, as he never said anything to *her*; in fact, his last remark was evidently addressed to a tree—so she stood and softly repeated to herself:—

> *'Humpty Dumpty sat on a wall:*
> *Humpty Dumpty had a great fall.*
> *All the King's horses and all the King's men*
> *Couldn't put Humpty Dumpty in his place again.'*

'That last line is much too long for the poetry,' she added, almost out loud, forgetting that Humpty Dumpty would hear her.

'Don't stand there chattering to yourself like that,' Humpty Dumpty said, looking at her for the first time, 'but tell me your name and your business.'

'My *name* is Alice, but—'

'It's a stupid enough name!' Humpty Dumpty interrupted impatiently. 'What does it mean?'

'*Must* a name mean something?' Alice asked

doubtfully.

'Of course it must,' Humpty Dumpty said with a short laugh: '*my* name means the shape I am—and a good handsome shape it is, too. With a name like yours, you might be any shape, almost.'

'Why do you sit out here all alone?' said Alice, not wishing to begin an argument.

'Why, because there's nobody with me!' cried Humpty Dumpty. 'Did you think I didn't know the answer to *that*? Ask another.'

'Don't you think you'd be safer down on the ground?' Alice went on, not with any idea of making another riddle, but simply in her good-natured anxiety for the queer creature. 'That wall is so *very* narrow!'

'What tremendously easy riddles you ask!' Humpty Dumpty growled out. 'Of course I don't think so! Why, if ever I *did* fall off—which there's no chance of—but *if* I did—' Here he pursed his lips and looked so solemn and grand that Alice could hardly help laughing. '*If* I did fall,' he went on, 'The King has promised me—with his very own mouth—to—to—'

'To send all his horses and all his men,' Alice interrupted, rather unwisely.

'Now I declare that's too bad!' Humpty Dumpty cried, breaking into a sudden passion. 'You've been listening at doors—and behind trees—and down

chimneys—or you couldn't have known it!'

'I haven't, indeed!' Alice said very gently. 'It's in a book.'

'Ah, well! They may write such things in a *book*,' Humpty Dumpty said in a calmer tone. 'That's what you call a History of England, that is. Now, take a good look at me! I'm one that has spoken to a King, *I* am: mayhap you'll never see such another: and to show you I'm not proud, you may shake hands with me!' And he grinned almost

from ear to ear, as he leant forwards (and as nearly as possible fell off the wall in doing so) and offered Alice his hand. She watched him a little anxiously as she took it. 'If he smiled much more, the ends of his mouth might meet behind,' she thought: 'and then I don't know what would happen to his head! I'm afraid it would come off!'

'Yes, all his horses and all his men,' Humpty Dumpty went on. 'They'd pick me up again in a minute, *they* would! However, this conversation is going on a little too fast: let's go back to the last remark but one.'

'I'm afraid I can't quite remember it,' Alice said very politely.

'In that case we start fresh,' said Humpty Dumpty, 'and it's my turn to choose a subject—' ('He talks about it just as if it was a game!' thought Alice.) 'So here's a question for you. How old did you say you were?'

Alice made a short calculation, and said 'Seven years and six months.'

'Wrong!' Humpty Dumpty exclaimed triumphantly. 'You never said a word like it!'

'I though you meant "How old *are* you?"' Alice explained.

'If I'd meant that, I'd have said it,' said Humpty Dumpty.

Alice didn't want to begin another argument, so she said nothing.

'Seven years and six months!' Humpty Dumpty repeated thoughtfully. 'An uncomfortable sort of age. Now if you'd asked *my* advice, I'd have said "Leave off at seven"—but it's too late now.'

'I never ask advice about growing,' Alice said indignantly.

'Too proud?' the other inquired.

Alice felt even more indignant at this suggestion. 'I mean,' she said, 'that one can't help growing older.'

'*One* can't, perhaps,' said Humpty Dumpty, 'but *two* can. With proper assistance, you might have left off at seven.'

'What a beautiful belt you've got on!' Alice suddenly remarked.

(They had had quite enough of the subject of age, she thought: and if they really were to take turns in choosing subjects, it was her turn now.) 'At least,' she corrected herself on second thoughts, 'a beautiful cravat, I should have said—no, a belt, I mean—I beg your pardon!' she added in dismay, for Humpty Dumpty looked thoroughly offended, and she began to wish she hadn't chosen that subject. 'If I only knew,' she thought to herself, 'which was neck and which was waist!'

Evidently Humpty Dumpty was very angry, though he said nothing for a minute or two. When he *did* speak again, it was in a deep growl.

'It is a—most—provoking—thing,' he said at last,

'when a person doesn't know a cravat from a belt!'

'I know it's very ignorant of me,' Alice said, in so humble a tone that Humpty Dumpty relented.

'It's a cravat, child, and a beautiful one, as you say. It's a present from the White King and Queen. There now!'

'Is it really?' said Alice, quite pleased to find that she *had* chosen a good subject, after all.

'They gave it me,' Humpty Dumpty continued thoughtfully, as he crossed one knee over the other and clasped his hands round it, 'they gave it me—for an un-birthday present.'

'I beg your pardon?' Alice said with a puzzled air.

'I'm not offended,' said Humpty Dumpty.

'I mean, what *is* an un-birthday present?'

'A present given when it isn't your birthday, of course.'

Alice considered a little. 'I like birthday presents best,' she said at last.

'You don't know what you're talking about!' cried Humpty Dumpty. 'How many days are there in a year?'

relent [rɪˈlɛnt] **v** 變溫和；變寬容

beg your pardon [bɛg] [jʊəˑ] [ˈpɑrdn] 請求原諒；不好意思，能再說一次嗎？（作者在此以這兩個語意玩起文字遊戲）

'Three hundred and sixty-five,' said Alice.

'And how many birthdays have you?'

'One.'

'And if you take one from three hundred and sixty-five, what remains?'

'Three hundred and sixty-four, of course.'

Humpty Dumpty looked doubtful. 'I'd rather see that done on paper,' he said.

Alice couldn't help smiling as she took out her memorandum-book, and worked the sum for him:

$$365$$
$$-\ \ 1$$
$$\overline{}$$
$$364$$

Humpty Dumpty took the book, and looked at it carefully. 'That seems to be done right—' he began.

'You're holding it upside down!' Alice interrupted.

'To be sure I was!' Humpty Dumpty said gaily, as she turned it round for him. 'I thought it looked a little queer. As I was saying, that *seems* to be done right—though I haven't time to look it over thoroughly just now—and that shows that there are three hundred and sixty-four days when you might get un-birthday presents—'

'Certainly,' said Alice.

'And only *one* for birthday presents, you know. There's glory for you!'

'I don't know what you mean by "glory,"' Alice said.

Humpty Dumpty smiled contemptuously. 'Of course you don't—till I tell you. I meant "there's a nice knock-down argument for you!"'

'But "glory" doesn't mean "a nice knock-down argument,"' Alice objected.

'When *I* use a word,' Humpty Dumpty said in rather a scornful tone, 'it means just what I choose it to mean—neither more nor less.'

'The question is,' said Alice, 'whether you *can* make words mean so many different things.'

'The question is,' said Humpty Dumpty, 'which is to be master—that's all.'

Alice was too much puzzled to say anything, so after a minute Humpty Dumpty began again. 'They've a temper, some of them—particularly verbs, they're the proudest—adjectives you can do anything with, but not verbs—however, *I* can manage the whole lot of them! Impenetrability! That's what *I* say!'

scornful ['skɔrnfəl] *adj* 輕蔑的，嘲笑的
impenetrability [ɪmˌpɛnətrə'bɪlətɪ] *n* 難以理解，費解

'Would you tell me, please,' said Alice 'what that means?'

'Now you talk like a reasonable child,' said Humpty Dumpty, looking very much pleased. 'I meant by "impenetrability" that we've had enough of that subject, and it would be just as well if you'd mention what you mean to do next, as I suppose you don't mean to stop here all the rest of your life.'

'That's a great deal to make one word mean,' Alice said in a thoughtful tone.

'When I make a word do a lot of work like that,' said Humpty Dumpty, 'I always pay it extra.'

'Oh!' said Alice. She was too much puzzled to make any other remark.

'Ah, you should see 'em come round me of a Saturday night,' Humpty Dumpty went on, wagging his head gravely from side to side: 'for to get their wages, you know.'

(Alice didn't venture to ask what he paid them with; and so you see I can't tell *you*.)

'You seem very clever at explaining words, Sir,' said Alice. 'Would you kindly tell me the meaning of the poem called "Jabberwocky"?'

'Let's hear it,' said Humpty Dumpty. 'I can explain all the poems that were ever invented—and a good many that haven't been invented just yet.'

This sounded very hopeful, so Alice repeated the first verse:

> *'Twas brillig, and the slithy toves*
> *Did gyre and gimble in the wabe;*
> *All mimsy were the borogoves,*
> *And the mome raths outgrabe.*

'That's enough to begin with,' Humpty Dumpty interrupted: 'there are plenty of hard words there. "*Brillig*" means four o'clock in the afternoon—the time when you begin *broiling* things for dinner.'

'That'll do very well,' said Alice: 'and "*slithy*"?'

'Well, "*slithy*" means "lithe and slimy." "Lithe" is the same as "active." You see it's like a portmanteau—there are two meanings packed up into one word.'

'I see it now,' Alice remarked thoughtfully: 'and what are "*toves*"?'

'Well, "*toves*" are something like badgers—they're something like lizards—and they're something like corkscrews.'

'They must be very curious looking creatures.'

'They are that,' said Humpty Dumpty: 'also they make their nests under sun-dials—also they live on cheese.'

'And what's the "*gyre*" and to "*gimble*"?'

'To "*gyre*" is to go round and round like a gyroscope. To "*gimble*" is to make holes like a gimlet.'

'And "*the wabe*" is the grass-plot round a sun-dial, I suppose?' said Alice, surprised at her own ingenuity.

'Of course it is. It's called "*wabe*," you know, because it goes a long way before it, and a long way behind it—'

'And a long way beyond it on each side,' Alice added.

'Exactly so. Well, then, "*mimsy*" is "flimsy and miserable" (there's another portmanteau for you). And a "*borogove*" is a thin shabby-looking bird with its feathers sticking out all round—something like a live mop.'

'And then "*mome raths*"?' said Alice. 'I'm afraid I'm giving you a great deal of trouble.'

'Well, a "*rath*" is a sort of green pig: but "*mome*" I'm not certain about. I think it's short for "from home"— meaning that they'd lost their way, you know.'

'And what does "*outgrabe*" mean?'

'Well, "*outgrabing*" is something between bellowing and whistling, with a kind of sneeze in the middle: however, you'll hear it done, maybe—down in the wood yonder—and when you've once heard it you'll be *quite*

gyroscope [ˈdʒaɪrəˌskop] **n** 陀螺儀；迴轉儀
ingenuity [ˌɪndʒəˈnuətɪ] **n** 聰明才智；足智多謀

content. Who's been repeating all that hard stuff to you?'

'I read it in a book,' said Alice. 'But I had some poetry repeated to me, much easier than that, by— Tweedledee, I think it was.'

'As to poetry, you know,' said Humpty Dumpty, stretching out one of his great hands, '*I* can repeat poetry as well as other folk, if it comes to that—'

'Oh, it needn't come to that!' Alice hastily said, hoping to keep him from beginning.

'The piece I'm going to repeat,' he went on without noticing her remark, 'was written entirely for your amusement.'

Alice felt that in that case she really *ought* to listen to it, so she sat down, and said 'Thank you' rather sadly.

> *In winter, when the fields are white,*
> *I sing this song for your delight—*

only I don't sing it,' he added, as an explanation.

'I see you don't,' said Alice.

'If you can *see* whether I'm singing or not, you've sharper eyes than most.' Humpty Dumpty remarked severely. Alice was silent.

> *In spring, when woods are getting green,*
> *I'll try and tell you what I mean.'*

'Thank you very much,' said Alice.

> *In summer, when the days are long,*
> *Perhaps you'll understand the song:*

> *In autumn, when the leaves are brown,*
> *Take pen and ink, and write it down.'*

'I will, if I can remember it so long,' said Alice.

'You needn't go on making remarks like that,' Humpty Dumpty said: 'they're not sensible, and they put me out.'

> *'I sent a message to the fish:*
> *I told them "This is what I wish."*

The little fishes of the sea,
They sent an answer back to me.

The little fishes' answer was
"We cannot do it, Sir, because—"'
'I'm afraid I don't quite understand,' said Alice.
'It gets easier further on,' Humpty Dumpty replied.
'I sent to them again to say
"It will be better to obey."

The fishes answered with a grin,
"Why, what a temper you are in!"

I told them once, I told them twice:
They would not listen to advice.

I took a kettle large and new,
Fit for the deed I had to do.

My heart went hop, my heart went thump;
I filled the kettle at the pump.

Then some one came to me and said,
"The little fishes are in bed."

I said to him, I said it plain,
"Then you must wake them up again."

I said it very loud and clear;
I went and shouted in his ear.'

Humpty Dumpty raised his voice almost to a scream as he repeated this verse, and Alice thought with a shudder, 'I wouldn't have been the messenger for *anything*!'

'But he was very stiff and proud;
He said "You needn't shout so loud!"

And he was very proud and stiff;
He said "I'd go and wake them, if—"

I took a corkscrew from the shelf:
I went to wake them up myself.

And when I found the door was locked,
I pulled and pushed and kicked and knocked.

And when I found the door was shut,
I tried to turn the handle, but—'

There was a long pause.

'Is that all?' Alice timidly asked.

'That's all,' said Humpty Dumpty. 'Good-bye.'

This was rather sudden, Alice thought: but, after such a *very* strong hint that she ought to be going, she felt that it would hardly be civil to stay. So she got up, and held out her hand. 'Good-bye, till we meet again!' she said as cheerfully as she could.

'I shouldn't know you again if we *did* meet,' Humpty

Dumpty replied in a discontented tone, giving her one of his fingers to shake; 'you're so exactly like other people.'

'The face is what one goes by, generally,' Alice remarked in a thoughtful tone.

'That's just what I complain of,' said Humpty Dumpty. 'Your face is the same as everybody has—the two eyes, so—' (marking their places in the air with this thumb) 'nose in the middle, mouth under. It's always the same. Now if you had the two eyes on the same side of the nose, for instance—or the mouth at the top—that would be *some* help.'

'It wouldn't look nice,' Alice objected. But Humpty Dumpty only shut his eyes and said 'Wait till you've tried.'

Alice waited a minute to see if he would speak again, but as he never opened his eyes or took any further notice of her, she said 'Good-bye!' once more, and, getting no answer to this, she quietly walked away: but she couldn't help saying to herself as she went, 'Of all the unsatisfactory—' (she repeated this aloud, as it was a great comfort to have such a long word to say) 'of all the unsatisfactory people I *ever* met—' She never finished the sentence, for at this moment a heavy crash shook the forest from end to end.

discontented [dɪskən'tɛntɪd] *adj* 不滿的

The Lion and the Unicorn

The next moment soldiers came running through the wood, at first in twos and threes, then ten or twenty together, and at last in such crowds that they seemed to fill the whole forest. Alice got behind a tree, for fear of being run over, and watched them go by.

She thought that in all her life she had never seen soldiers so uncertain on their feet: they were always tripping over something or other, and

whenever one went down, several more always fell over him, so that the ground was soon covered with little heaps of men.

Then came the horses. Having four feet, these managed rather better than the foot-soldiers: but even *they* stumbled now and then; and it seemed to be a regular rule that, whenever a horse stumbled the rider fell off instantly. The confusion got worse every moment, and Alice was very glad to get out of the wood into an open place, where she found the White King seated on the ground, busily writing in his memorandum-book.

'I've sent them all!' the King cried in a tone of delight, on seeing Alice. 'Did you happen to meet any soldiers, my dear, as you came through the wood?'

'Yes, I did,' said Alice: 'several thousand, I should think.'

'Four thousand two hundred and seven, that's the exact number,' the King said, referring to his book. 'I couldn't send all the horses, you know, because two of them are wanted in the game. And I haven't sent the two Messengers, either. They're both gone to the town. Just look along the road, and tell me if you can see either of them.'

'I see nobody on the road,' said Alice.

'I only wish *I* had such eyes,' the King remarked in a

fretful tone. 'To be able to see Nobody! And at that distance, too! Why, it's as much as *I* can do to see real people, by this light!'

All this was lost on Alice, who was still looking intently along the road, shading her eyes with one hand. 'I see somebody now!' she exclaimed at last. 'But he's coming very slowly—and what curious attitudes he goes into!' (For the messenger kept skipping up and down, and wriggling like an eel, as he came along, with his great hands spread out like fans on each side.)

'Not at all,' said the King. 'He's an Anglo-Saxon Messenger—and those are Anglo-Saxon attitudes. He only does them when he's happy. His name is Haigha.' (He pronounced it so as to rhyme with 'mayor.')

'I love my love with an H,' Alice couldn't help beginning, 'because he is Happy. I hate him with an H, because he is Hideous. I fed him with—with—with Ham-sandwiches and Hay. His name is Haigha, and he lives—'

'He lives on the Hill,' the King remarked simply, without the least idea that he was joining in the game, while Alice was still hesitating for the name of a town beginning with

fretful [ˈfrɛtfl] *adj* 煩惱的，焦躁的
intently [ɪnˈtɛntlɪ] *adv* 專心地，專注地

H. 'The other Messenger's called Hatta. I must have *two*, you know—to come and go. One to come, and one to go.'

'I beg your pardon?' said Alice.

'It isn't respectable to beg,' said the King.

'I only meant that I didn't understand,' said Alice. 'Why one to come and one to go?'

'Didn't I tell you?' the King repeated impatiently. 'I must have *two*—to fetch and carry. One to fetch, and one to carry.'

At this moment the Messenger arrived: he was far too much out of breath to say a word, and could only wave his hands about, and make the most fearful faces at the poor King.

'This young lady loves you with an H,' the King said, introducing Alice in the hope of turning off the Messenger's attention from himself—but it was no use—the Anglo-Saxon attitudes only got more extraordinary every moment, while the great eyes rolled wildly from side to side.

'You alarm me!' said the King. 'I feel faint—Give me a ham sandwich!'

On which the Messenger, to Alice's great amusement, opened a bag that hung round his neck, and handed a sandwich to the King, who devoured it greedily.

devour [dɪˈvaʊr] **v** 狼吞虎嚥地吃，吃光

'Another sandwich!' said the King.

'There's nothing but hay left now,' the Messenger said, peeping into the bag.

'Hay, then,' the King murmured in a faint whisper.

Alice was glad to see that it revived him a good deal. 'There's nothing like eating hay when you're faint,' he remarked to her, as he munched away.

'I should think throwing cold water over you would

revive [rɪˈvaɪv] **v** 使甦醒；使復甦

be better,' Alice suggested: 'or some sal-volatile.'

'I didn't say there was nothing *better*,' the King replied. 'I said there was nothing *like* it.' Which Alice did not venture to deny.

'Who did you pass on the road?' the King went on, holding out his hand to the Messenger for some more hay.

'Nobody,' said the Messenger.

'Quite right,' said the King: 'this young lady saw him too. So of course Nobody walks slower than you.'

'I do my best,' the Messenger said in a sulky tone. 'I'm sure nobody walks much faster than I do!'

'He can't do that,' said the King, 'or else he'd have been here first. However, now you've got your breath, you may tell us what's happened in the town.'

'I'll whisper it,' said the Messenger, putting his hands to his mouth in the shape of a trumpet, and stooping so as to get close to the King's ear. Alice was sorry for this, as she wanted to hear the news too. However, instead of whispering, he simply shouted at the top of his voice 'They're at it again!'

'Do you call *that* a whisper?' cried the poor King, jumping up and shaking himself. 'If you do such a thing again, I'll have you buttered! It went through and through my head like an earthquake!'

'It would have to be a very tiny earthquake!' thought Alice. 'Who are at it again?' she ventured to ask.

'Why the Lion and the Unicorn, of course,' said the King.

'Fighting for the crown?'

'Yes, to be sure,' said the King: 'and the best of the joke is, that it's *my* crown all the while! Let's run and see them.' And they trotted off, Alice repeating to herself, as she ran, the words of the old song:—

> '*The Lion and the Unicorn were fighting for the crown:*
> *The Lion beat the Unicorn all round the town.*
> *Some gave them white bread, some gave them brown;*
> *Some gave them plum-cake and drummed them out of town.*'

'Does—the one—that wins—get the crown?' she asked, as well as she could, for the run was putting her quite out of breath.

'Dear me, no!' said the King. 'What an idea!'

'Would you—be good enough,' Alice panted out, after running a little further, 'to stop a minute—just to get—one's breath again?'

'I'm *good* enough,' the King said, 'only I'm not strong enough. You see, a minute goes by so fearfully quick. You might as well try to stop a Bandersnatch!'

Alice had no more breath for talking, so they trotted on in silence, till they came in sight of a great crowd, in the middle of which the Lion and Unicorn were fighting. They were in such a cloud of dust, that at first Alice could not make out which was which: but she soon managed to

distinguish the Unicorn by his horn.

They placed themselves close to where Hatta, the other messenger, was standing watching the fight, with a cup of tea in one hand and a piece of bread-and-butter in the other.

'He's only just out of prison, and he hadn't finished his tea when he was sent in,' Haigha whispered to Alice: 'and they only give them oyster-shells in there—so you see he's very hungry and thirsty. How are you, dear child?' he

distinguish [dɪˈstɪŋgwɪʃ] **v** 辨認出

went on, putting his arm affectionately round Hatta's neck.

Hatta looked round and nodded, and went on with his bread and butter.

'Were you happy in prison, dear child?' said Haigha.

Hatta looked round once more, and this time a tear or two trickled down his cheek: but not a word would he say.

'Speak, can't you!' Haigha cried impatiently. But Hatta only munched away, and drank some more tea.

'Speak, won't you!' cried the King. 'How are they getting on with the fight?'

Hatta made a desperate effort, and swallowed a large piece of bread-and-butter. 'They're getting on very well,' he said in a choking voice: 'each of them has been down about eighty-seven times.'

'Then I suppose they'll soon bring the white bread and the brown?' Alice ventured to remark.

'It's waiting for 'em now,' said Hatta: 'this is a bit of it as I'm eating.'

There was a pause in the fight just then, and the Lion and the Unicorn sat down, panting, while the King called out 'Ten minutes allowed for refreshments!' Haigha and Hatta set to work at once, carrying rough trays of white and brown bread. Alice took a piece to taste, but it was *very* dry.

'I don't think they'll fight any more to-day,' the King said to Hatta: 'go and order the drums to begin.' And Hatta went bounding away like a grasshopper.

For a minute or two Alice stood silent, watching him. Suddenly she brightened up. 'Look, look!' she cried, pointing eagerly. 'There's the White Queen running across the country! She came flying out of the wood over yonder—How fast those Queens *can* run!'

'There's some enemy after her, no doubt,' the King said, without even looking round. 'That wood's full of them.'

'But aren't you going to run and help her?' Alice asked, very much surprised at his taking it so quietly.

'No use, no use!' said the King. 'She runs so fearfully quick. You might as well try to catch a Bandersnatch! But I'll make a memorandum about her, if you like—She's a dear good creature,' he repeated softly to himself, as he opened his memorandum-book. 'Do you spell "creature" with a double "e"?'

At this moment the Unicorn sauntered by them, with his hands in his pockets. 'I had the best of it this time?' he said to the King, just glancing at him as he passed.

'A little—a little,' the King replied, rather nervously. 'You shouldn't have run him through with your horn, you know.'

'It didn't hurt him,' the Unicorn said carelessly, and he

saunter [ˈsɒntə] **v** 閒逛；漫步

was going on, when his eye happened to fall upon Alice: he turned round rather instantly, and stood for some time looking at her with an air of the deepest disgust.

'What—is—this?' he said at last.

'This is a child!' Haigha replied eagerly, coming in front of Alice to introduce her, and spreading out both his hands towards her in an Anglo-Saxon attitude. 'We only found it to-day. It's as large as life, and twice as natural!'

'I always thought they were fabulous monsters!' said the Unicorn. 'Is it alive?'

'It can talk,' said Haigha, solemnly.

The Unicorn looked dreamily at Alice, and said 'Talk, child.'

Alice could not help her lips curling up into a smile as she began: 'Do you know, I always thought Unicorns were fabulous monsters, too! I never saw one alive before!'

'Well, now that we *have* seen each other,' said the Unicorn, 'if you'll believe in me, I'll believe in you. Is that a bargain?'

'Yes, if you like,' said Alice.

'Come, fetch out the plum-cake, old man!' the Unicorn went on, turning from her to the King. 'None of your brown bread for me!'

'Certainly—certainly!' the King muttered, and beckoned to Haigha. 'Open the bag!' he whispered. 'Quick! Not that one—that's full of hay!'

Haigha took a large cake out of the bag, and gave it to Alice to hold, while he got out a dish and carving-knife. How they all came out of it Alice couldn't guess. It was just like a conjuring-trick, she thought.

The Lion had joined them while this was going on: he looked very tired and sleepy, and his eyes were half shut. 'What's this!' he said, blinking lazily at Alice, and speaking in a deep hollow tone that sounded like the tolling of a great bell.

conjuring ['kʌndʒərɪŋ] *n* 魔術

'Ah, what *is* it, now?' the Unicorn cried eagerly. 'You'll never guess! *I* couldn't.'

The Lion looked at Alice wearily. 'Are you animal—vegetable—or mineral?' he said, yawning at every other word.

'It's a fabulous monster!' the Unicorn cried out, before Alice could reply.

'Then hand round the plum-cake, Monster,' the Lion said, lying down and putting his chin on his paws. 'And sit down, both of you,' (to the King and the Unicorn): 'fair play with the cake, you know!'

The King was evidently very uncomfortable at having to sit down between the two great creatures; but there was no other place for him.

'What a fight we might have for the crown, *now*!' the Unicorn said, looking slyly up at the crown, which the poor King was nearly shaking off his head, he trembled so much.

'I should win easy,' said the Lion.

'I'm not so sure of that,' said the Unicorn.

'Why, I beat you all round the town, you chicken!' the Lion replied angrily, half getting up as he spoke.

Here the King interrupted, to prevent the quarrel going on: he was very nervous, and his voice quite quivered. 'All round the town?' he said. 'That's a good long way. Did you go by the old bridge, or the market-place? You get the best view by the old bridge.'

'I'm sure I don't know,' the Lion growled out as he lay

down again. 'There was too much dust to see anything. What a time the Monster is, cutting up that cake!'

Alice had seated herself on the bank of a little brook, with the great dish on her knees, and was sawing away diligently with the knife. 'It's very provoking!' she said, in reply to the Lion (she was getting quite used to being called 'the Monster'). 'I've cut several slices already, but they always join on again!'

'You don't know how to manage Looking-glass cakes,' the Unicorn remarked. 'Hand it round first, and cut it afterwards.'

This sounded nonsense, but Alice very obediently got up, and carried the dish round, and the cake divided itself into three pieces as she did so. '*Now* cut it up,' said the Lion, as she returned to her place with the empty dish.

'I say, this isn't fair!' cried the Unicorn, as Alice sat with the knife in her hand, very much puzzled how to begin. 'The Monster has given the Lion twice as much as me!'

'She's kept none for herself, anyhow,' said the Lion. 'Do you like plum-cake, Monster?'

But before Alice could answer him, the drums began.

Where the noise came from, she couldn't make out:

diligently [ˈdɪlədʒəntlɪ] *adv* 勤勉地；認真地

the air seemed full of it, and it rang through and through her head till she felt quite deafened. She started to her feet and sprang across the little brook in her terror,

♠　♥　♣　♦

and had just time to see the Lion and the Unicorn rise to their feet, with angry looks at being interrupted in their feast, before she dropped to her knees, and put her hands over her ears, vainly trying to shut out the dreadful uproar.

'If *that* doesn't "drum them out of town,"' she thought to herself, 'nothing ever will!'

08 /

'It's My Own Invention'

After a while the noise seemed gradually to die away, till all was dead silence, and Alice lifted up her head in some alarm. There was no one to be seen, and her first thought was that she must have been dreaming about the Lion and the Unicorn and those queer Anglo-Saxon Messengers. However, there was the great dish still lying at her feet, on which she had tried to cut the plum-cake, 'So I wasn't dreaming, after all,' she said to herself, 'unless—unless we're all part of the same dream. Only I do hope it's *my* dream, and not the Red King's! I don't like belonging to another person's dream,' she went on in a rather complaining tone: 'I've a great mind to go and wake him, and see what happens!'

At this moment her thoughts were interrupted by a loud shouting of 'Ahoy! Ahoy! Check!' and a Knight dressed in crimson armour came galloping down upon

her, brandishing a great club. Just as he reached her, the horse stopped suddenly: 'You're my prisoner!' the Knight cried, as he tumbled off his horse.

Startled as she was, Alice was more frightened for him than for herself at the moment, and watched him with some anxiety as he mounted again. As soon as he was comfortably in the saddle, he began once more 'You're my—' but here another voice broke in 'Ahoy! Ahoy! Check!' and Alice looked round in some surprise for the new enemy.

This time it was a White Knight. He drew up at Alice's side, and tumbled off his horse just as the Red Knight had done: then he got on again, and the two Knights sat and looked at each other for some time without speaking. Alice looked from one to the other in some bewilderment.

'She's *my* prisoner, you know!' the Red Knight said at last.

'Yes, but then *I* came and rescued her!' the White Knight replied.

'Well, we must fight for her, then,' said the Red Knight, as he took up his helmet (which hung from the

brandish ['brændɪʃ] *v* 揮舞
bewilderment [bɪ'wɪldə-mənt] *n* 迷惑：昏亂

saddle, and was something the shape of a horse's head), and put it on.

'You will observe the Rules of Battle, of course?' the White Knight remarked, putting on his helmet too.

'I always do,' said the Red Knight, and they began banging away at each other with such fury that Alice got behind a tree to be out of the way of the blows.

'I wonder, now, what the Rules of Battle are,' she said to herself, as she watched the fight, timidly peeping out from her hiding-place: 'one Rule seems to be, that if one

Knight hits the other, he knocks him off his horse, and if he misses, he tumbles off himself—and another Rule seems to be that they hold their clubs with their arms, as if they were Punch and Judy—What a noise they make when they tumble! Just like a whole set of fire-irons falling into the fender! And how quiet the horses are! They let them get on and off them just as if they were tables!'

Another Rule of Battle, that Alice had not noticed, seemed to be that they always fell on their heads, and the battle ended with their both falling off in this way, side by side: when they got up again, they shook hands, and then the Red Knight mounted and galloped off.

'It was a glorious victory, wasn't it?' said the White Knight, as he came up panting.

'I don't know,' Alice said doubtfully. 'I don't want to be anybody's prisoner. I want to be a Queen.'

'So you will, when you've crossed the next brook,' said the White Knight. 'I'll see you safe to the end of the wood—and then I must go back, you know. That's the end of my move.'

'Thank you very much,' said Alice. 'May I help you off with your helmet?' It was evidently more than he could manage by himself; however, she managed to shake him out of it at last.

'Now one can breathe more easily,' said the Knight, putting back his shaggy hair with both hands, and turning

his gentle face and large mild eyes to Alice. She thought she had never seen such a strange-looking soldier in all her life.

He was dressed in tin armour, which seemed to fit him very badly, and he had a queer-shaped little deal box fastened across his shoulder, upside-down, and with the lid hanging open. Alice looked at it with great curiosity.

'I see you're admiring my little box.' the Knight said in a friendly tone. 'It's my own invention—to keep clothes and sandwiches in. You see I carry it upside-down, so that the rain can't get in.'

'But the things can get *out*,' Alice gently remarked. 'Do you know the lid's open?'

'I didn't know it,' the Knight said, a shade of vexation passing over his face. 'Then all the things must have fallen out! And the box is no use without them.' He unfastened it as he spoke, and was just going to throw it into the bushes, when a sudden thought seemed to strike him, and he hung it carefully on a tree. 'Can you guess why I did that?' he said to Alice.

Alice shook her head.

'In hopes some bees may make a nest in it—then I should get the honey.'

'But you've got a bee-hive—or something like one—fastened to the saddle,' said Alice.

'Yes, it's a very good bee-hive,' the Knight said in a discontented tone, 'one of the best kind. But not a single bee has come near it yet. And the other thing is a mouse-trap. I suppose the mice keep the bees out—or the bees keep the mice out, I don't know which.'

'I was wondering what the mouse-trap was for,' said Alice. 'It isn't very likely there would be any mice on the horse's back.'

'Not very likely, perhaps,' said the Knight: 'but if they *do* come, I don't choose to have them running all about.'

'You see,' he went on after a pause, 'it's as well to be provided for *everything*. That's the reason the horse has all

those anklets round his feet.'

'But what are they for?' Alice asked in a tone of great curiosity.

'To guard against the bites of sharks,' the Knight replied. 'It's an invention of my own. And now help me on. I'll go with you to the end of the wood—What's the dish for?'

'It's meant for plum-cake,' said Alice.

'We'd better take it with us,' the Knight said. 'It'll come in handy if we find any plum-cake. Help me to get it into this bag.'

This took a very long time to manage, though Alice held the bag open very carefully, because the Knight was so *very* awkward in putting in the dish: the first two or three times that he tried he fell in himself instead. 'It's rather a tight fit, you see,' he said, as they got it in a last; 'There are so many candlesticks in the bag.' And he hung it to the saddle, which was already loaded with bunches of carrots, and fire-irons, and many other things.

'I hope you've got your hair well fastened on?' he continued, as they set off.

'Only in the usual way,' Alice said, smiling.

'That's hardly enough,' he said, anxiously. 'You see the wind is so *very* strong here. It's as strong as soup.'

'Have you invented a plan for keeping the hair from being blown off?' Alice enquired.

'Not yet,' said the Knight. 'But I've got a plan for keeping it from *falling* off.'

'I should like to hear it, very much.'

'First you take an upright stick,' said the Knight. 'Then you make your hair creep up it, like a fruit-tree. Now the reason hair falls off is because it hangs *down*— things never fall *upwards*, you know. It's a plan of my own invention. You may try it if you like.'

It didn't sound a comfortable plan, Alice thought, and for a few minutes she walked on in silence, puzzling over the idea, and every now and then stopping to help the poor Knight, who certainly was *not* a good rider.

Whenever the horse stopped (which it did very often), he fell off in front; and whenever it went on again (which it generally did rather suddenly), he fell off behind. Otherwise he kept on pretty well, except that he had a habit of now and then falling off sideways; and as he generally did this on the side on which Alice was walking, she soon found that it was the best plan not to walk *quite* close to the horse.

'I'm afraid you've not had much practice in riding,' she ventured to say, as she was helping him up from his fifth tumble.

The Knight looked very much surprised, and a little offended at the remark. 'What makes you say that?' he asked, as he scrambled back into the saddle, keeping hold of Alice's hair with one hand, to save himself from falling

over on the other side.

'Because people don't fall off quite so often, when they've had much practice.'

'I've had plenty of practice,' the Knight said very gravely: 'plenty of practice!'

Alice could think of nothing better to say than 'Indeed?' but she said it as heartily as she could. They went on a little way in silence after this, the Knight with his eyes shut, muttering to himself, and Alice watching anxiously for the next tumble.

'The great art of riding,' the Knight suddenly began in a loud voice, waving his right arm as he spoke, 'is to keep—' Here the sentence ended as suddenly as it had begun, as the Knight fell heavily on the top of his head exactly in the path where Alice was walking. She was quite frightened this time, and said in an anxious tone, as she picked him up, 'I hope no bones are broken?'

'None to speak of,' the Knight said, as if he didn't mind breaking two or three of them. 'The great art of riding, as I was saying, is—to keep your balance properly. Like this, you know—'

He let go the bridle, and stretched out both his arms to show Alice what he meant, and this time he fell flat on his back, right under the horse's feet.

'Plenty of practice!' he went on repeating, all the time that Alice was getting him on his feet again. 'Plenty of

practice!'

'It's too ridiculous!' cried Alice, losing all her patience this time. 'You ought to have a wooden horse on wheels, that you ought!'

'Does that kind go smoothly?' the Knight asked in a tone of great interest, clasping his arms round the horse's neck as he spoke, just in time to save himself from tumbling off again.

'Much more smoothly than a live horse,' Alice said, with a little scream of laughter, in spite of all she could do to prevent it.

'I'll get one,' the Knight said thoughtfully to himself. 'One or two—several.'

There was a short silence after this, and then the Knight went on again. 'I'm a great hand at inventing things. Now, I daresay you noticed, that last time you picked me up, that I was looking rather thoughtful?'

'You *were* a little grave,' said Alice.

'Well, just then I was inventing a new way of getting over a gate—would you like to hear it?'

'Very much indeed,' Alice said politely.

'I'll tell you how I came to think of it,' said the Knight. 'You see, I said to myself, "The only difficulty is with the feet: the *head* is high enough already." Now, first I put my head on the top of the gate—then I stand on my head—then the feet are high enough, you see—then I'm over, you see.'

'Yes, I suppose you'd be over when that was done,' Alice said thoughtfully: 'but don't you think it would be rather hard?'

'I haven't tried it yet,' the Knight said, gravely: 'so I can't tell for certain—but I'm afraid it *would* be a little hard.'

He looked so vexed at the idea, that Alice changed the subject hastily. 'What a curious helmet you've got!' she said cheerfully. 'Is that your invention too?'

The Knight looked down proudly at his helmet, which hung from the saddle. 'Yes,' he said, 'but I've invented a better one than that—like a sugar loaf. When I used to wear it, if I fell off the horse, it always touched the ground directly. So I had a *very* little way to fall, you see—But there *was* the danger of falling *into* it, to be sure. That happened to me once—and the worst of it was, before I could get out again, the other White Knight came and put it on. He thought it was his own helmet.'

The knight looked so solemn about it that Alice did not dare to laugh. 'I'm afraid you must have hurt him,' she said in a trembling voice, 'being on the top of his head.'

'I had to kick him, of course,' the Knight said, very seriously. 'And then he took the helmet off again—but it took hours and hours to get me out. I was as fast as—as lightning, you know.'

'But that's a different kind of fastness,' Alice objected.

The Knight shook his head. 'It was all kinds of

fastness with me, I can assure you!' he said. He raised his hands in some excitement as he said this, and instantly rolled out of the saddle, and fell headlong into a deep ditch.

Alice ran to the side of the ditch to look for him. She was rather startled by the fall, as for some time he had kept on very well, and she was afraid that he really *was* hurt this time. However, though she could see nothing but the soles of his feet, she was much relieved to hear that he was talking on in his usual tone. 'All kinds of fastness,' he repeated: 'but it was careless of him to put another man's helmet on—with the man in it, too.'

'How *can* you go on talking so quietly, head downwards?' Alice asked, as she dragged him out by the feet, and laid him in a heap on the bank.

The Knight looked surprised at the question. 'What does it matter where my body happens to be?' he said. 'My mind goes on working all the same. In fact, the more head downwards I am, the more I keep inventing new things.'

'Now the cleverest thing of the sort that I ever did,' he went on after a pause, 'was inventing a new pudding during the meat-course.'

'In time to have it cooked for the next course?' said Alice. 'Well, not the *next* course,' the Knight said in a slow thoughtful tone: 'no, certainly not the next *course*.'

'Then it would have to be the next day. I suppose you wouldn't have two pudding-courses in one dinner?'

'Well, not the *next* day,' the Knight repeated as before: 'not the next *day*. In fact,' he went on, holding his head down, and his voice getting lower and lower, 'I don't believe that pudding ever *was* cooked! In fact, I don't believe that pudding ever *will* be cooked! And yet it was a very clever pudding to invent.'

'What did you mean it to be made of?' Alice asked, hoping to cheer him up, for the poor Knight seemed quite low-spirited about it.

'It began with blotting paper,' the Knight answered with a groan.

'That wouldn't be very nice, I'm afraid—'

'Not very nice *alone*,' he interrupted, quite eagerly: 'but you've no idea what a difference it makes mixing it

with other things—such as gunpowder and sealing-wax. And here I must leave you.' They had just come to the end of the wood.

Alice could only look puzzled: she was thinking of the pudding.

'You are sad,' the Knight said in an anxious tone: 'let me sing you a song to comfort you.'

'Is it very long?' Alice asked, for she had heard a good deal of poetry that day.

'It's long,' said the Knight, 'but very, *very* beautiful. Everybody that hears me sing it—either it brings the *tears* into their eyes, or else—'

'Or else what?' said Alice, for the Knight had made a sudden pause.

'Or else it doesn't, you know. The name of the song is called "*Haddocks' Eyes*."'

'Oh, that's the name of the song, is it?' Alice said, trying to feel interested.

'No, you don't understand,' the Knight said, looking a little vexed. 'That's what the name is *called*. The name really *is* "*The Aged Aged Man*."'

'Then I ought to have said "That's what the *song* is called"?' Alice corrected herself.

'No, you oughtn't: that's quite another thing! The *song* is called "*Ways and Means*": but that's only what it's *called*, you know!'

'Well, what *is* the song, then?' said Alice, who was by this time completely bewildered.

'I was coming to that,' the Knight said. 'The song really *is* "*A-sitting On A Gate*": and the tune's my own invention.'

So saying, he stopped his horse and let the reins fall on its neck: then, slowly beating time with one hand, and with a faint smile lighting up his gentle foolish face, as if he enjoyed the music of his song, he began.

Of all the strange things that Alice saw in her journey Through The Looking-Glass, this was the one that she always remembered most clearly. Years afterwards she could bring the whole scene back again, as if it had been only yesterday—the mild blue eyes and kindly smile of the Knight—the setting sun gleaming through his hair, and shining on his armour in a blaze of light that quite dazzled her—the horse quietly moving about, with the reins hanging loose on his neck, cropping the grass at her feet—and the black shadows of the forest behind—all this she took in like a picture, as, with one hand shading her eyes, she leant against a tree, watching the strange pair, and listening, in a half dream, to the melancholy music of the song.

gleam [glim] **v** 發微光；閃爍

'But the tune *isn't* his own invention,' she said to herself: 'it's "I give thee all, I can no more."' She stood and listened very attentively, but no tears came into her eyes.

> *I'll tell thee everything I can;*
> *There's little to relate.*
> *I saw an aged aged man,*
> *A-sitting on a gate.*
> *"Who are you, aged man?" I said,*
> *"and how is it you live?"*
> *And his answer trickled through my head*
> *Like water through a sieve.*
>
> *He said "I look for butterflies*
> *That sleep among the wheat:*
> *I make them into mutton-pies,*
> *And sell them in the street.*
> *I sell them unto men," he said,*
> *"Who sail on stormy seas;*
> *And that's the way I get my bread—*
> *A trifle, if you please."*
>
> *But I was thinking of a plan*
> *To dye one's whiskers green,*
> *And always use so large a fan*
> *That they could not be seen.*
> *So, having no reply to give*

To what the old man said,
I cried, "Come, tell me how you live!"
And thumped him on the head.

His accents mild took up the tale:
He said "I go my ways,
And when I find a mountain-rill,
I set it in a blaze;
And thence they make a stuff they call
Rolands' Macassar Oil—
Yet twopence-halfpenny is all
They give me for my toil."

But I was thinking of a way
To feed oneself on batter,
And so go on from day to day
Getting a little fatter.
I shook him well from side to side,
Until his face was blue:
"Come, tell me how you live," I cried,
"And what it is you do!"

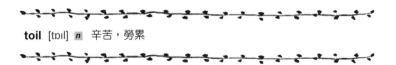

toil [tɔɪl] *n* 辛苦，勞累

'It's My Own Invention'

He said "I hunt for haddocks' eyes
Among the heather bright,
And work them into waistcoat-buttons
In the silent night.
And these I do not sell for gold
Or coin of silvery shine
But for a copper halfpenny,
And that will purchase nine.

"I sometimes dig for buttered rolls,
Or set limed twigs for crabs;
I sometimes search the grassy knolls
For wheels of Hansom-cabs.
And that's the way" (he gave a wink)
"By which I get my wealth—
And very gladly will I drink
Your Honour's noble health."

I heard him then, for I had just
Completed my design
To keep the Menai bridge from rust
By boiling it in wine.
I thanked him much for telling me
The way he got his wealth,
But chiefly for his wish that he
Might drink my noble health.

And now, if e'er by chance I put
My fingers into glue
Or madly squeeze a right-hand foot
Into a left-hand shoe,
Or if I drop upon my toe
A very heavy weight,
I weep, for it reminds me so,
Of that old man I used to know—

Whose look was mild, whose speech was slow,
Whose hair was whiter than the snow,
Whose face was very like a crow,
With eyes, like cinders, all aglow,
Who seemed distracted with his woe,
Who rocked his body to and fro,
And muttered mumblingly and low,
As if his mouth were full of dough,
Who snorted like a buffalo—
That summer evening, long ago,
A-sitting on a gate.'

As the Knight sang the last words of the ballad, he gathered up the reins, and turned his horse's head along the road by which they had come. 'You've only a few yards to go,' he said, 'down the hill and over that little brook, and then you'll be a Queen—But you'll stay and see me off first?' he added as Alice turned with an eager look in the direction to which he pointed. 'I shan't be long. You'll wait and wave your handkerchief when I get to that turn in the road? I think it'll encourage me, you see.'

'Of course I'll wait,' said Alice: 'and thank you very much for coming so far—and for the song—I liked it very much.'

'I hope so,' the Knight said doubtfully: 'but you didn't cry so much as I thought you would.'

So they shook hands, and then the Knight rode slowly away into the forest. 'It won't take long to see him *off*, I expect,' Alice said to herself, as she stood watching him. 'There he goes! Right on his head as usual! However, he gets on again pretty easily—that comes of having so many things hung round the horse—' So she went on talking to herself, as she watched the horse walking leisurely along the road, and the Knight tumbling off, first on one side and then on the other. After the fourth or fifth tumble he reached the turn, and then she waved her handkerchief to him, and waited till he was out of sight.

'I hope it encouraged him,' she said, as she turned to run down the hill: 'and now for the last brook, and to be a Queen! How grand it sounds!' A very few steps brought her to the edge of the brook. 'The Eighth Square at last!' she cried as she bounded across,

and threw herself down to rest on a lawn as soft as moss, with little flower-beds dotted about it here and there. 'Oh, how glad I am to get here! And what *is* this on my head?' she exclaimed in a tone of dismay, as she put her hands up to something very heavy, and fitted tight all round her head.

'But how *can* it have got there without my knowing

it?' she said to herself, as she lifted it off, and set it on her lap to make out what it could possibly be.

It was a golden crown.

09 /

Queen Alice

'Well, this *is* grand!' said Alice. 'I never expected I should be a Queen so soon—and I'll tell you what it is, your majesty,' she went on in a severe tone (she was always rather fond of scolding herself), 'it'll never do for you to be lolling about on the grass like that! Queens have to be dignified, you know!'

So she got up and walked about—rather stiffly just at first, as she was afraid that the crown might come off: but she comforted herself with the thought that there was nobody to see her, 'and if I really am a Queen,' she said as she sat down again, 'I shall be able to manage it quite well in time.'

Everything was happening so oddly that she didn't

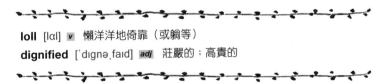

loll [lɑl] **v** 懶洋洋地倚靠（或躺等）
dignified [ˈdɪgnəˌfaɪd] **adj** 莊嚴的；高貴的

feel a bit surprised at finding the Red Queen and the White Queen sitting close to her, one on each side: she would have liked very much to ask them how they came there, but she feared it would not be quite civil. However, there would be no harm, she thought, in asking if the game was over. 'Please, would you tell me—' she began, looking timidly at the Red Queen.

'Speak when you're spoken to!' The Queen sharply interrupted her.

'But if everybody obeyed that rule,' said Alice, who was always ready for a little argument, 'and if you only spoke when you were spoken to, and the other person always waited for *you* to begin, you see nobody would ever say anything, so that—'

'Ridiculous!' cried the Queen. 'Why, don't you see, child—' here she broke off with a frown, and, after thinking for a minute, suddenly changed the subject of the conversation. 'What do you mean by "If you really are a Queen"? What right have you to call yourself so? You can't be a Queen, you know, till you've passed the proper examination. And the sooner we begin it, the better.'

'I only said "if"!' poor Alice pleaded in a piteous tone.

The two Queens looked at each other, and the Red Queen remarked, with a little shudder, 'She *says* she only said "if"—'

'But she said a great deal more than that!' the White Queen moaned, wringing her hands. 'Oh, ever so much more than that!'

'So you did, you know,' the Red Queen said to Alice. 'Always speak the truth—think before you speak—and write it down afterwards.'

'I'm sure I didn't mean—' Alice was beginning, but the Red Queen interrupted her impatiently.

'That's just what I complain of! You *should* have meant! What do you suppose is the use of child without any meaning? Even a joke should have some meaning—

piteous ['pɪtɪəs] *adj* 令人憐憫的

and a child's more important than a joke, I hope. You couldn't deny that, even if you tried with both hands.'

'I don't deny things with my *hands*,' Alice objected.

'Nobody said you did,' said the Red Queen. 'I said you couldn't if you tried.'

'She's in that state of mind,' said the White Queen, 'that she wants to deny *something*—only she doesn't know what to deny!'

'A nasty, vicious temper,' the Red Queen remarked; and then there was an uncomfortable silence for a minute or two.

The Red Queen broke the silence by saying to the White Queen, 'I invite you to Alice's dinner-party this afternoon.'

The White Queen smiled feebly, and said 'And I invite *you*.'

'I didn't know I was to have a party at all,' said Alice; 'but if there is to be one, I think *I* ought to invite the guests.'

'We gave you the opportunity of doing it,' the Red Queen remarked: 'but I daresay you've not had many lessons in manners yet?'

'Manners are not taught in lessons,' said Alice. 'Lessons

vicious [ˈvɪʃəs] *adj* 卑劣的；邪惡的；墮落的

teach you to do sums, and things of that sort.'

'And you do Addition?' the White Queen asked. 'What's one and one and one and one and one and one and one and one and one and one?'

'I don't know,' said Alice. 'I lost count.'

'She can't do Addition,' the Red Queen interrupted. 'Can you do Subtraction? Take nine from eight.'

'Nine from eight I can't, you know,' Alice replied very readily: 'but—'

'She can't do Subtraction,' said the White Queen. 'Can you do Division? Divide a loaf by a knife—what's the answer to that?'

'I suppose—' Alice was beginning, but the Red Queen answered for her. 'Bread-and-butter, of course. Try another Subtraction sum. Take a bone from a dog: what remains?'

Alice considered. 'The bone wouldn't remain, of course, if I took it—and the dog wouldn't remain; it would come to bite me—and I'm sure *I* shouldn't remain!'

'Then you think nothing would remain?' said the Red Queen.

'I think that's the answer.'

'Wrong, as usual,' said the Red Queen: 'the dog's temper would remain.'

'But I don't see how—'

'Why, look here!' the Red Queen cried. 'The dog would lose its temper, wouldn't it?'

'Perhaps it would,' Alice replied cautiously.

'Then if the dog went away, its temper would remain!' the Queen exclaimed triumphantly.

Alice said, as gravely as she could, 'They might go different ways.' But she couldn't help thinking to herself, 'What dreadful nonsense we *are* talking!'

'She can't do sums a *bit*!' the Queens said together, with great emphasis.

'Can *you* do sums?' Alice said, turning suddenly on the White Queen, for she didn't like being found fault with so much.

The Queen gasped and shut her eyes. 'I can do Addition, if you give me time—but I can't do Subtraction, under *any* circumstances!'

'Of course you know your A B C?' said the Red Queen.

'To be sure I do.' said Alice.

'So do I,' the White Queen whispered: 'we'll often say it over together, dear. And I'll tell you a secret—I can read words of one letter! Isn't *that* grand! However, don't be discouraged. You'll come to it in time.'

Here the Red Queen began again. 'Can you answer useful questions?' she said. 'How is bread made?'

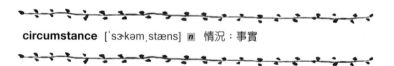

circumstance ['sɝkəm‚stæns] **n** 情況：事實

'I know *that*!' Alice cried eagerly. 'You take some flour—'

'Where do you pick the flower?' the White Queen asked. 'In a garden, or in the hedges?'

'Well, it isn't *picked* at all,' Alice explained: 'it's *ground*—'

'How many acres of ground?' said the White Queen. 'You mustn't leave out so many things.'

'Fan her head!' the Red Queen anxiously interrupted. 'She'll be feverish after so much thinking.' So they set to work and fanned her with bunches of leaves, till she had to beg them to leave off, it blew her hair about so.

'She's all right again now,' said the Red Queen. 'Do you know Languages? What's the French for fiddle-de-dee?'

'Fiddle-de-dee's not English,' Alice replied gravely.

'Who ever said it was?' said the Red Queen.

Alice thought she saw a way out of the difficulty this time. 'If you'll tell me what language "fiddle-de-dee" is, I'll tell you the French for it!' she exclaimed triumphantly.

flour [flaʊr] *n* 麵粉（發音似 **flower**，因而下一段白棋王后把「麵粉」聽成了「花朵」）

ground [graʊnd] *v* 碾磨 *n* 田地（作者在此以這兩個語意玩起文字遊戲）

But the Red Queen drew herself up rather stiffly, and said 'Queens never make bargains.'

'I wish Queens never asked questions,' Alice thought to herself.

'Don't let us quarrel,' the White Queen said in an anxious tone. 'What is the cause of lightning?'

'The cause of lightning,' Alice said very decidedly, for she felt quite certain about this, 'is the thunder—no, no!' she hastily corrected herself. 'I meant the other way.'

'It's too late to correct it,' said the Red Queen: 'when you've once said a thing, that fixes it, and you must take the consequences.'

'Which reminds me—' the White Queen said, looking down and nervously clasping and unclasping her hands, 'we had *such* a thunderstorm last Tuesday—I mean one of the last set of Tuesdays, you know.'

Alice was puzzled. 'In *our* country,' she remarked, 'there's only one day at a time.'

The Red Queen said, 'That's a poor thin way of doing things. Now *here*, we mostly have days and nights two or three at a time, and sometimes in the winter we take as many as five nights together—for warmth, you know.'

'Are five nights warmer than one night, then?' Alice ventured to ask.

'Five times as warm, of course.'

'But they should be five times as *cold*, by the same

rule—'

'Just so!' cried the Red Queen. 'Five times as warm, *and* five times as cold—just as I'm five times as rich as you are, *and* five times as clever!'

Alice sighed and gave it up. 'It's exactly like a riddle with no answer!' she thought.

'Humpty Dumpty saw it too,' the White Queen went on in a low voice, more as if she were talking to herself. 'He came to the door with a corkscrew in his hand—'

'What did he want?' said the Red Queen.

'He said he *would* come in,' the White Queen went on, 'because he was looking for a hippopotamus. Now, as it happened, there wasn't such a thing in the house, that morning.'

'Is there generally?' Alice asked in an astonished tone.

'Well, only on Thursdays,' said the Queen.

'I know what he came for,' said Alice: 'he wanted to punish the fish, because—'

Here the White Queen began again. 'It was *such* a thunderstorm, you can't think!' ('She *never* could, you know,' said the Red Queen.) 'And part of the roof came off, and ever so much thunder got in—and it went rolling round the room in great lumps—and knocking over the tables and things—till I was so frightened, I couldn't remember my own name!'

Alice thought to herself, 'I never should *try* to

remember my name in the middle of an accident! Where would be the use of it?' but she did not say this aloud, for fear of hurting the poor Queen's feeling.

'Your Majesty must excuse her,' the Red Queen said to Alice, taking one of the White Queen's hands in her own, and gently stroking it: 'she means well, but she can't help saying foolish things, as a general rule.'

The White Queen looked timidly at Alice, who felt she *ought* to say something kind, but really couldn't think of anything at the moment.

'She never was really well brought up,' the Red Queen went on: 'but it's amazing how good-tempered she is! Pat her on the head, and see how pleased she'll be!' But this was more than Alice had courage to do.

'A little kindness—and putting her hair in papers— would do wonders with her—'

The White Queen gave a deep sigh, and laid her head on Alice's shoulder. 'I *am* so sleepy?' she moaned.

'She's tired, poor thing!' said the Red Queen. 'Smooth her hair—lend her your nightcap—and sing her a soothing lullaby.'

'I haven't got a nightcap with me,' said Alice, as she tried to obey the first direction: 'and I don't know any soothing lullabies.'

'I must do it myself, then,' said the Red Queen, and she began:

> *'Hush-a-by lady, in Alice's lap!*
> *Till the feast's ready, we've time for a nap:*
> *When the feast's over, we'll go to the ball—*
> *Red Queen, and White Queen, and Alice, and all!*

'And now you know the words,' she added, as she put her head down on Alice's other shoulder, 'just sing it through to *me*. I'm getting sleepy, too.' In another moment both Queens were fast asleep, and snoring loud.

'What *am* I to do?' exclaimed Alice, looking about in great perplexity, as first one round head, and then the other, rolled down from her shoulder, and lay like a heavy

perplexity [pə'plɛksɪtɪ] *n* 困惑，茫然

lump in her lap. 'I don't think it *ever* happened before, that any one had to take care of two Queens asleep at once! No, not in all the History of England—it couldn't, you know, because there never was more than one Queen at a time. Do wake up, you heavy things!' she went on in an impatient tone; but there was no answer but a gentle snoring.

The snoring got more distinct every minute, and sounded more like a tune: at last she could even make out the words, and she listened so eagerly that, when the two great heads vanished from her lap, she hardly missed them.

She was standing before an arched doorway over which were the words QUEEN ALICE in large letters, and on each side of the arch there was a bell-handle; one was marked 'Visitors' Bell,' and the other 'Servants' Bell.'

'I'll wait till the song's over,' thought Alice, 'and then I'll ring—the—*which* bell must I ring?' she went on, very much puzzled by the names. 'I'm not a visitor, and I'm not a servant. *There ought* to be one marked "Queen," you know—'

Just then the door opened a little way, and a creature with a long beak put its head out for a moment and said 'No admittance till the week after next!' and shut the door again with a bang.

distinct [dɪ'stɪŋkt] *adj* 明顯的，清楚的

Alice knocked and rang in vain for a long time, but at last, a very old Frog, who was sitting under a tree, got up and hobbled slowly towards her: he was dressed in bright yellow, and had enormous boots on.

'What is it, now?' the Frog said in a deep hoarse whisper.

Alice turned round, ready to find fault with anybody. 'Where's the servant whose business it is to answer the door?' she began angrily.

'Which door?' said the Frog.

Alice almost stamped with irritation at the slow drawl in which he spoke. '*This* door, of course!'

The Frog looked at the door with his large dull eyes for a minute: then he went nearer and rubbed it with his thumb, as if he were trying whether the paint would come off; then he looked at Alice.

'To answer the door?' he said. 'What's it been asking of?' He was so hoarse that Alice could scarcely hear him.

'I don't know what you mean,' she said.

'I talks English, doesn't I?' the Frog went on. 'Or are you deaf? What did it ask you?'

'Nothing!' Alice said impatiently. 'I've been knocking at it!'

'Shouldn't do that—shouldn't do that—' the Frog muttered. 'Vexes it, you know.' Then he went up and gave the door a kick with one of his great feet. 'You let *it* alone,' he panted out, as he hobbled back to his tree, 'and it'll let *you* alone, you know.'

At this moment the door was flung open, and a shrill voice was heard singing:

> *'To the Looking-Glass world it was Alice that said,*

irritation [ˌɪrəˈteʃən] *n* 惱怒，生氣

"I've a sceptre in hand, I've a crown on my head;
Let the Looking-Glass creatures, whatever they be,
Come and dine with the Red Queen, the White Queen, and me."'

And hundreds of voices joined in the chorus:

'Then fill up the glasses as quick as you can,
And sprinkle the table with buttons and bran:
Put cats in the coffee, and mice in the tea—
And welcome Queen Alice with thirty-times-three!'

Then followed a confused noise of cheering, and
Alice thought to herself, 'Thirty times three makes ninety.
I wonder if any one's counting?' In a minute there was
silence again, and the same shrill voice sang another verse;

"'O Looking-Glass creatures," quoth Alice, "draw near!
'Tis an honour to see me, a favour to hear:
'Tis a privilege high to have dinner and tea
Along with the Red Queen, the White Queen, and me!"'

Then came the chorus again:—

'Then fill up the glasses with treacle and ink,
Or anything else that is pleasant to drink:
Mix sand with the cider, and wool with the wine—
And welcome Queen Alice with ninety-times-nine!'

'Ninety times nine!' Alice repeated in despair, 'Oh,
that'll never be done! I'd better go in at once—' and there
was a dead silence the moment she appeared.

Alice glanced nervously along the table, as she walked
up the large hall, and noticed that there were about fifty

guests, of all kinds: some were animals, some birds, and there were even a few flowers among them. 'I'm glad they've come without waiting to be asked,' she thought: 'I should never have known who were the right people to invite!'

There were three chairs at the head of the table; the Red and White Queens had already taken two of them, but the middle one was empty. Alice sat down in it, rather uncomfortable in the silence, and longing for some one to speak.

At last the Red Queen began. 'You've missed the soup and fish,' she said. 'Put on the joint!' And the waiters set a leg of mutton before Alice, who looked at it rather anxiously, as she had never had to carve a joint before.

'You look a little shy; let me introduce you to that leg of mutton,' said the Red Queen. 'Alice—Mutton; Mutton—Alice.' The leg of mutton got up in the dish and made a little bow to Alice; and Alice returned the bow, not knowing whether to be frightened or amused.

'May I give you a slice?' she said, taking up the knife and fork, and looking from one Queen to the other.

'Certainly not,' the Red Queen said, very decidedly: 'it isn't etiquette to cut any one you've been introduced to. Remove the joint!' And the waiters carried it off, and brought a large plum-pudding in its place.

'I won't be introduced to the pudding, please,' Alice said rather hastily, 'or we shall get no dinner at all. May I give you some?'

But the Red Queen looked sulky, and growled 'Pudding—Alice; Alice—Pudding. Remove the pudding!' and the waiters took it away so quickly that Alice couldn't return its bow.

However, she didn't see why the Red Queen should be the only one to give orders, so, as an experiment, she called out 'Waiter! Bring back the pudding!' and there it was again in a moment like a conjuring-trick. It was so large that she couldn't help feeling a *little* shy with it, as she had been with the mutton; however, she conquered her shyness by a great effort and cut a slice and handed it to the Red Queen.

'What impertinence!' said the Pudding. 'I wonder how you'd like it, if I were to cut a slice out of *you*, you creature!'

etiquette [ˈɛtɪkɛt] **n** 禮節；禮儀
impertinence [ɪmˈpɜtnəns] **n** 無禮

It spoke in a thick, suety sort of voice, and Alice hadn't a word to say in reply: she could only sit and look at it and gasp.

'Make a remark,' said the Red Queen: 'it's ridiculous to leave all the conversation to the pudding!'

'Do you know, I've had such a quantity of poetry repeated to me to-day,' Alice began, a little frightened at finding that, the moment she opened her lips, there was dead silence, and all eyes were fixed upon her; 'and it's a very curious thing, I think—every poem was about fishes in some way. Do you know why they're so fond of fishes, all about here?'

She spoke to the Red Queen, whose answer was a little wide of the mark. 'As to fishes,' she said, very slowly and solemnly, putting her mouth close to Alice's ear, 'her White Majesty knows a lovely riddle—all in poetry—all about fishes. Shall she repeat it?'

'Her Red Majesty's very kind to mention it,' the White Queen murmured into Alice's other ear, in a voice like the cooing of a pigeon. 'It would be *such* a treat! May I?'

'Please do,' Alice said very politely.

The White Queen laughed with delight, and stroked Alice's cheek. Then she began:

'"First, the fish must be caught."
That is easy: a baby, I think, could have caught it.
"Next, the fish must be bought."
That is easy: a penny, I think, would have bought it.

"Now cook me the fish!"
That is easy, and will not take more than a minute.
"Let it lie in a dish!"
That is easy, because it already is in it.

"Bring it here! Let me sup!"
It is easy to set such a dish on the table.
"Take the dish-cover up!"
Ah, that is so hard that I fear I'm unable!

For it holds it like glue—
Holds the lid to the dish, while it lies in the middle:
Which is easiest to do,
Un-dish-cover the fish, or dishcover the riddle?'

'Take a minute to think about it, and then guess,' said the Red Queen. 'Meanwhile, we'll drink your health— Queen Alice's health!' she screamed at the top of her voice, and all the guests began drinking it directly, and very queerly they managed it: some of them put their glasses upon their heads like extinguishers, and drank all that trickled down their faces—others upset the decanters, and drank the wine as it ran off the edges of the table— and three of them (who looked like kangaroos) scrambled into the dish of roast mutton, and began eagerly lapping up the gravy, 'just like pigs in a trough!' thought Alice.

'You ought to return thanks in a neat speech,' the Red

Queen said, frowning at Alice as she spoke.

'We must support you, you know,' the White Queen whispered, as Alice got up to do it, very obediently, but a little frightened.

'Thank you very much,' she whispered in reply, 'but I can do quite well without.'

'That wouldn't be at all the thing,' the Red Queen said very decidedly: so Alice tried to submit to it with a good grace.

('And they *did* push so!' she said afterwards, when she was telling her sister the history of the feast. 'You would have thought they wanted to squeeze me flat!')

In fact it was rather difficult for her to keep in her place while she made her speech: the two Queens pushed her so, one on each side, that they nearly lifted her up into the air: 'I rise to return thanks——' Alice began: and she really *did* rise as she spoke, several inches; but she got hold of the edge of the table, and managed to pull herself down again.

'Take care of yourself!' screamed the White Queen, seizing Alice's hair with both her hands. 'Something's going to happen!'

And then (as Alice afterwards described it) all sorts of things happened in a moment. The candles all grew up to the ceiling, looking something like a bed of rushes with fireworks at the top. As to the bottles, they each took a pair

of plates, which they hastily fitted on as wings, and so, with forks for legs, went fluttering about in all directions: 'and very like birds they look,' Alice thought to herself, as well as she could in the dreadful confusion that was beginning.

At this moment she heard a hoarse laugh at her side, and turned to see what was the matter with the White Queen; but, instead of the Queen, there was the leg of mutton sitting in the chair. 'Here I am!' cried a voice from the soup tureen, and Alice turned again, just in time to see the Queen's broad good-natured face grinning at her for a moment over the edge of the tureen, before she disappeared into the soup.

There was not a moment to be lost. Already several of the guests were lying down in the dishes, and the soup ladle was walking up the table towards Alice's chair, and beckoning to her impatiently to get out of its way.

'I can't stand this any longer!' she cried as she jumped up and seized the table-cloth with both hands: one good pull, and plates, dishes, guests, and candles came crashing down together in a heap on the floor.

'And as for *you*,' she went on, turning fiercely upon the Red Queen, whom she considered as the cause of all the mischief—but the Queen was no longer at her side—

beckon ['bɛkŋ] **v** （招手或點頭）向……示意；召喚

she had suddenly dwindled down to the size of a little doll, and was now on the table, merrily running round and round after her own shawl, which was trailing behind her.

At any other time, Alice would have felt surprised at this, but she was far too much excited to be surprised at anything *now*. 'As for *you*,' she repeated, catching hold of the little creature in the very act of jumping over a bottle which had just lighted upon the table, 'I'll shake you into a kitten, that I will!'

dwindle ['dwɪndl] *v* 變小；漸漸減少

10 /

Shaking

She took her off the table as she spoke, and shook her backwards and forwards with all her might.

The Red Queen made no resistance whatever; only her face grew very small, and her eyes got large and green: and still, as Alice went on shaking her, she kept on growing shorter—and fatter—and softer—and rounder—and—

11 /
Waking

—and it really *was* a kitten, after all.

12 /

Which Dreamed it?

'Your majesty shouldn't purr so loud,' Alice said, rubbing her eyes, and addressing the kitten, respectfully, yet with some severity. 'You woke me out of oh! such a nice dream! And you've been along with me, Kitty—all through the Looking-Glass world. Did you know it, dear?'

It is a very inconvenient habit of kittens (Alice had once made the remark) that, whatever you say to them, they *always* purr. 'If they would only purr for "yes" and mew for "no," or any rule of that sort,' she had said, 'so that one could keep up a conversation! But how *can* you talk with a person if they always say the same thing?'

On this occasion the kitten only purred: and it was impossible to guess whether it meant 'yes' or 'no.'

So Alice hunted among the chessmen on the table till

severity [səˈvɛrətɪ] *n* 嚴肅

she had found the Red Queen: then she went down on her knees on the hearth-rug, and put the kitten and the Queen to look at each other. 'Now, Kitty!' she cried, clapping her hands triumphantly. 'Confess that was what you turned into!'

('But it wouldn't look at it,' she said, when she was explaining the thing afterwards to her sister: 'it turned away its head, and pretended not to see it: but it looked a *little* ashamed of itself, so I think it *must* have been the Red Queen.')

'Sit up a little more stiffly, dear!' Alice cried with a merry laugh. 'And curtsey while you're thinking what to— what to purr. It saves time, remember!' And she caught it up and gave it one little kiss, 'just in honour of having been a Red Queen.'

'Snowdrop, my pet!' she went on, looking over her shoulder at the White Kitten, which was still patiently undergoing its toilet, 'when *will* Dinah have finished with your White Majesty, I wonder? That must be the reason you were so untidy in my dream—Dinah! do you know that you're scrubbing a White Queen? Really, it's most disrespectful of you!

stiffly [ˈstɪflɪ] _adv_ 直挺挺地；堅硬地

'And what did *Dinah* turn to, I wonder?' she prattled on, as she settled comfortably down, with one elbow in the rug, and her chin in her hand, to watch the kittens. 'Tell me, Dinah, did you turn to Humpty Dumpty? I *think* you did—however, you'd better not mention it to your friends just yet, for I'm not sure.

prattle ['prætl] **v** 小孩般說話；嘰嘰喳喳地說

'By the way, Kitty, if only you'd been really with me in my dream, there was one thing you *would* have enjoyed—I had such a quantity of poetry said to me, all about fishes! To-morrow morning you shall have a real treat. All the time you're eating your breakfast, I'll repeat "The Walrus and the Carpenter" to you; and then you can make believe it's oysters, dear!

'Now, Kitty, let's consider who it was that dreamed it all. This is a serious question, my dear, and you should *not* go on licking your paw like that—as if Dinah hadn't washed you this morning! You see, Kitty, it *must* have been either me or the Red King. He was part of my dream, of course—but then I was part of his dream, too! *Was* it the Red King, Kitty? You were his wife, my dear, so you ought to know—Oh, Kitty, *do* help to settle it! I'm sure your paw can wait!' But the provoking kitten only began on the other paw, and pretended it hadn't heard the question.

Which do *you* think it was?

> *A boat beneath a sunny sky,*
> *Lingering onward dreamily*
> *In an evening of July—*

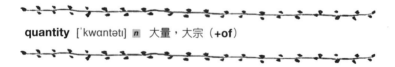

quantity [ˈkwɑntətɪ] *n* 大量，大宗（**+of**）

Children three that nestle near,
Eager eye and willing ear,
Pleased a simple tale to hear—

Long has paled that sunny sky:
Echoes fade and memories die.
Autumn frosts have slain July.

Still she haunts me, phantomwise,
Alice moving under skies
Never seen by waking eyes.

Children yet, the tale to hear,
Eager eye and willing ear,
Lovingly shall nestle near.

In a Wonderland they lie,
Dreaming as the days go by,
Dreaming as the summers die:

Ever drifting down the stream—
Lingering in the golden gleam—
Life, what is it but a dream?